THE HEALER

THE HEALER

KELLY LYNN COLBY

Copyright © 2022 by Kelly Lynn Colby

Cursed Dragon Ship Publishing, LLC

6046 FM 2920 Rd, #231, Spring, TX 77379

captwyvern@curseddragonship.com

Cover © 2022 by Stefanie Saw

Copy Edit by S.G. George

ISBN 978-1-951445-35-5

ISBN 978-1-951445-36-2 (ebook)

All rights reserved

No part of this book may be reproduced in any form or by any electronic or mechanical means, including information storage and retrieval systems, without written permission from the publisher, except for the use of brief quotations in a book review.

This books is a work of fiction fresh from the author's imagination. Any resemblance to actual persons or places is mere coincidence.

To my father, Roger Johnson, I feel your memory everywhere.

Chapter One

Even the sun thought it was too early as it lingered below the horizon, hesitant to rise. Why had Flores grabbed me at the crack of dawn to consult on an old case involving a man sentenced to life in prison? Admittedly, Huntsville was over an hour away, but that still put us there around 7 a.m. Over the last few months, we'd worked together to solve a few cold cases. I totally pictured the buddy cop television version of our adventures. Detective Mateo Flores, hardcore seeker of truth and justice, and Fauna Young, empath with comic relief potential, strive to find justice for long suffering families.

We'd never ventured out this damn early though.

Behind the wheel, Flores looked just as put together as he would if it were a decent hour. He wore a nice suit, more expensive than most underpaid cops due to Austin's insistence, and his hair had the fresh-out-of-military-service trim. Meanwhile, I'd slipped on a button-up and jeans. I didn't know what the proper attire for a prison visit entailed. My gloves snugly covered my hands, though. My support group of empaths had helped me overcome much of my fear over other people's emotions, as well as showing me how to separate myself with preparation and mental tools instead of protective clothing. Yet, I hadn't quite mastered those techniques. And a prison surely held extreme levels of emotional baggage from current and past residents that I really didn't want to experience if I could avoid it.

Actually, I needed to think about something else before my own anxiety countered all of my shaky protections. "Flores?"

"Yes?" His deep voice alone offered some comfort.

"I thought the crack of dawn was just a saying, a metaphor for the beginning of a new day."

"And?"

I gestured to the dark, early morning sky that seemed to be split at the horizon by an orange glow. "But it's a literal interpretation of the cracked sky in the dawn."

Flores's fingers drummed on the steering wheel. "That's what I see every morning on my run through Memorial Park. Though I never saw it quite so violently before."

"You run this early in the morning? What happened to you when you were a child? There's got to be help out there."

My sarcasm fell flat. Flores stared out the window, and I felt an air of fear—and maybe regret?—with a slight tightening of my stomach. I'd gotten better at blocking Flores's personal emotions as I'd spent more time with him and sort of adjusted to his frequency. Either what he was feeling now was super strong or my own morning routine of meditation and centering really did work and I was off balance because I'd skipped it.

Judging by his solid gaze out the window, it might be a bit of both. Should I probe more or leave it all for the consultation? Even though I knew Flores believed in my abilities, I still had that imposter syndrome where I wanted to make sure no one told me too much so when I did read a memory or a person, they'd know it was truly what I experienced. So weird to think like that when I didn't use my abilities for anything beyond helping Flores and catching a thief or two at my store. Old habits, I supposed.

As we exited 610 and merged onto 45 North heading to Huntsville, I couldn't help but wonder what we'd talk about for the long drive. But I couldn't just sit here, or I'd fall asleep and truly not be ready to read the inmate for Flores.

Come to think of it, he hadn't really told me much about what we were heading into. "What kind of early visiting hours does the prison have?"

"I set an appointment to meet with him outside of hours." His lip quirked up just barely, and I felt the air relax around him. "There are some perks to being an HPD detective."

"Perks?" My mood rose with his, and I vowed to keep it there. "I'd prefer a free meal from Jus' Mac or a meatball sub from Crisp. Now those would be perks."

With a raised eyebrow, Flores glimpsed my way. "You didn't have time for breakfast, did you?"

"Well, if I'm ever awake at this hour, it's coming home quite drunk, and all I want are pancakes."

He nodded. "I know just the place. We'll hit the Woodlands on the way back."

"Perfect." We were back on track. Should I risk it by asking about the man I was meant to read? "So, this prisoner I'm about to meet, I'm confused on what you need me for exactly. You've never brought me to a live witness or suspect before, it's always been boxed evidence to see if I could sense any impressions on them. I have zero experience questioning a suspect." Well, as far as Flores knew anyway. Some secrets deserved to stay buried.

Flores guffawed, one harsh sound, gruffer than I think he intended. "Without Collins as the bad cop, I'm not sure how far we'd get."

"So why do you need me for this? Obviously, the criminal has been caught. It's not an unsolved case."

I didn't see emotions as colors, but I bet if I did, the waves flowing off of Flores would be in constant flux as his feelings swirled uncentered and undecided. It wasn't unpleasant to experience because nothing stayed long enough to leave a strong, dominating impression. Whatever this was all about, it had Flores in turmoil.

I had to let him know I supported him regardless. "Look. Whatever it is, I've got your back. I'd simply like to be better prepared when I face whatever it is I'm about to face. Like I don't even know his name. It is a him, right? Do they have a female prison in Huntsville?"

"Not anymore." Flores switched lanes for no reason I could discern. I guessed he needed to do something to distract part of his brain. As the waves from him calmed down, it seemed to work. "You said you can tell when people are lying, like a lie detector."

That was the part of my life I tried to forget. Being able to tell when someone was lying versus telling the truth was only the beginning. I'd gotten good enough to interpret a target's emotional reactions so specifically I was able to guide questions to manipulate them. At least now I understood why Flores was so nervous. He was prepared to ask me to do something he knew I was extremely uncomfortable with. Was I ready? Had I worked on my own guilt enough, paid enough back to society with a few good deeds? Who was I to decide when I'd done enough?

Whatever this case was, it was obviously important to Flores; yet, he hadn't dragged me out as soon as he believed my abilities were real. Maybe he thought I was ready. Was his belief in me enough?

"Better than a lie detector. I can also tell you what they're truly feeling. You're not going to get a false reading with me."

"That's why we can't use—" His vibrating phone interrupted him. He glanced at the older model stuck by a magnet to his dash. I could probably get him a deal for the new one. "It's 1200 Travis."

The job never let him rest for long. I could never form a romantic relationship with a cop. Their hours were too unpredictable, and I was too needy. How Austin managed a marriage with Flores I'd never know.

Flores's face fell as the voice on the other end filled him in. After he hung up, he said, "We'll have to reschedule. I have a call at San Jacinto and Prairie."

For a detective, "a call" meant a dead body.

Chapter Two

My shoulder ached as I remembered my personal brush with a murderer last year. After the brutalized victims I'd witnessed, I had no desire to repeat the experience. Not only had I lived through my own vicious attack, but I had also touched those victims and fell into their assaults. Even though it was only memories I experienced, I wasn't eager to see another dead body in real life. Never again would be too soon.

After making his turn, Flores sped down the road much faster than I was comfortable with. My hands caressed the seatbelt as if to assure my aching anxiety I was safe.

His deep voice relieved my frozen terror. "I'll drop you off first."

Come on, Fauna. Put on your big girl panties. How many serial killers could there have been hunting empaths in this world? I was safe. "No, you don't have to." I almost sounded confident. "I'll grab an Uber from downtown."

"Are you sure?" Flores's hands hovered over the blinker as we approached the exit to my side of town.

"Of course I am."

He still seemed indecisive. I had to give him something

more. "Don't try to read my emotions. That's my area. Just trust my words and get to your crime scene. I can take care of myself, you know."

Without further argument, Flores returned both hands to the wheel and passed the 610 exit. The emotions that had hovered around him as we headed to Huntsville faded to a slight vibration I could no longer sense without physical contact. I'd witnessed this a few times; it was his game face, emotionally anyway. His actual face always looked serious and focused. If I couldn't sense the swells of emotional reaction underneath, I would think he didn't feel anything at all. Being an empath really helped one not judge a book by its cover.

After the initial shock wore off, I pondered what Flores was about to deal with. The map of downtown ran through my head. "Isn't that by St. Benedict's?"

Smoothly crossing four lanes of light traffic, Flores made the next exit. "It is."

"Gina volunteers there all the time. Amelia and I helped when we were in college for a class, but Gina stuck with it."

I tried not to feel guilty for not continuing, but Gina wasn't an empath. The mentally ill among the homeless tortured me with their uncontrolled emotions and deep pain. Families on hard times offered their own torment as their hopelessness and frustration bled into my own mind. And the addicts. Sometimes, they were a barrel of laughs and I didn't even need to drink, other times, so depressed and desperate I wasn't sure how they were able to walk. I was an emotional wreck while we volunteered at the shelter.

It occurred to me I'd never explained my erratic behavior to my two best friends. Now that they knew about my empathic abilities, I suppose I could clear it all up. Maybe I could even volunteer with Gina occasionally, since I could shield myself from so much that I couldn't manage before.

"You know the drill," Flores said as he swung his car next to two marked vehicles with their lights flashing. "You can't say a thing until the information has been released to the public."

"Yes, sir." I barely managed to not salute him.

He straightened his jacket and badge around his neck. As he exited, Flores paused and looked at me. "You're sure you're okay."

I held up my phone with the Uber app open. "I think I can handle it."

With a quick nod, he marched to the scene with that sexy, confident walk I found so attractive. Too bad he didn't play for my team. For a split second, I thought about texting Tucker who was the star player on my team. Then thought better of it. At this time of the morning, he was either starting his shift at the hospital or ending one. I'd catch up with him later.

After moving a bit away from the scene to make sure the Uber driver could find me without running into a blockade, I ordered my ride. While I waited, I paced in front of the waist-high wall that separated the shelter from the street. Calling St. Benedict's a shelter wasn't descriptive enough. They offered phones and computers to contact relatives, services for job searches and training, washers and dryers to clean clothes, doctors and psychiatrists, and of course, food and water. This organization wasn't a place to hide the homeless; it was a place that attempted to help them.

A glance at the doorway where Flores talked with Detective Collins brought a fresh bout of guilt. This close to St. Benedict's there was typically a spattering of people who had nowhere else to go when the shelter was full. I had no idea what had caused the death of the victim Flores inspected, but I'd be willing to bet it was neglect of one form or another. I wondered if Gina knew the person. Come to think of it, where *was* the waiting crowd? They must have scattered when the police showed.

My feet worked a slight oval around the intersection. I didn't want to sit on the wall. I didn't know who was there last or if their emotions were strong enough to leave anything behind.

THE HEALER

Next time Flores set an early meetup, I swore to give myself more time before joining him. Apparently, missing my meditation to center myself was not an option anymore. I felt more out of sorts and unfiltered than I had since the Collected, the empath group Albert Johnson had assembled, taught me tricks to protect my sanity from my ability without hiding in my house, at Chipped, or—well there was no way to mask it or make it sound better—in a bottle. At times like these, my traitorous mind felt cursed.

A silver Toyota Corolla with a U sticker in the window pulled up at the next cross section. Since it was the same vehicle described by the app, I figured he didn't want to get stuck in traffic by the scene. Fine by me. I started to jog across the street to meet him when a familiar feeling shocked me to a halt.

What was that? It was so strong, for a moment I thought someone stood in the bushes.

The driver rolled down his window and shouted, "Are you Fauna?"

I wanted to ignore the odd sensation and just move on, but it was like I was frozen in place. Whatever had been left behind wasn't an impression, not a memory, but something else, like a combination of thoughts and emotions unique to a person, a very familiar person. I'd never felt anything like it.

The part I couldn't shake was the familiarity. Whoever left this bit of themselves behind was very close to me, yet distant. Like I used to know them, but it had been a while. I could only come up with one person who fit that bill. But it couldn't be him. I mean, he said he'd never come back. Houston was mine. He promised.

Even if he had come back, why would he be here? Altruism was certainly not his game. Was he homeless now and looking for help? Maybe the impression was left years ago. It was not like I'd been down here in a long time. I couldn't estimate its staying power. My legs picked up speed to sprint to my ride.

Plus, it was a large city. The odds of me running into him

were tiny, even if he broke his promise and returned. I'd just need to stay away from this block. Flores hadn't yet asked for my help on a fresh case after what happened last year. I was relatively sure he wouldn't need me for whatever tragedy ended the life of the person in the alley.

Something inside made me stop with my hand on the car door handle. A glance over my shoulder gave me no clues on what Flores had found. It was better I didn't know. I nodded to the driver as I buckled my seatbelt. I'd never been more grateful for the app communicating my destination for me. I couldn't trust my voice right now.

My life was going so well. He couldn't be back.

Chapter Three

The townhouse smelled incredible as the marinated skirt steak sizzled on the grill pan. The too-loud music battled with the vent fan for dominance, canceling out any other sound—such as knocking on the door. Which was why I felt the presence of Gina and Amelia before I heard them. They'd been my closest friends since college, and their typical swirl of emotions were as familiar to me as my own. Though there seemed to be a bit more stress mixed in today.

The entire experience made me ponder the thing I felt in the street. Maybe I had felt such a thing before, but only when the people were actually present. When Gina and Amelia left, their familiar emotional signature left with them. Why then would one get left behind? I downed the last swallow of cab from my well-used glass. I'd deal with that later, or not at all if I could manage.

Gina blew me an air kiss as she tossed her thick jacket on the back of the couch and pulled the wine out of its Spec's bag. With her hands firmly over her ears, Amelia aimed for the Bluetooth speaker and turned down my Billy Joel.

I flipped the steak for a quick sear on the opposite side. "Hey, I was enjoying that."

Amelia's short-cropped hair danced over her ears as she shook her head at me. "Were you? It sounded more like you were trying to drown out a listening device."

"Hahaha, you're so witty." I flipped the fan off and plopped the steak onto the cutting board to rest. "Y'all are early. I still need to warm up the tortillas."

Gina grabbed two stemmed glasses from under the modest kitchen island. "I need to start drinking now."

That explained the extra stress in the air. Gina was never the first of us to open a bottle. "What happened?"

A quick shake of the opened cab bottle on the counter told Amelia it was already empty. So she pulled the corkscrew from its magnet on the wall and tossed it to Gina.

Gina's ponytail danced as she caught the tool and set it aside. With a simple twist, she opened the mixed red she'd brought and poured a bit in each glass. Oh, it was going to be one of those nights. Before saying a word, Gina gulped most of her glass down and refilled it.

As I toasted a tortilla in a dry pan, I exchanged a worried glance with Amelia. With school in session, Gina usually kept her drinking to a minimum. She never wanted to show up hungover to her second-grade students.

Amelia handed me my refilled glass. "It was a rough day."

Before I could ask for details, Gina explained, "One of the most dedicated volunteers at St. Benedict's, Robert Morris, was found dead in an alley behind the main building."

My cheeks flushed. "Flores was called to a scene at that location this morning."

Gina sat up straight. "Were you with him? What happened? Rob was adored by the homeless population. No one cared more or did more for them. He was unmarried with no children. His entire life was about improving the living conditions of Houston's homeless. It's so tragic."

I took a moment to feel relief that the emotional signature left at the scene wasn't the dead body. I'd never met Robert

Morris. Amelia took my empty glass for a refill. I didn't even remember draining it. Both of my friends stared at me, waiting for an answer. I was grateful they knew about my ability after years of keeping it secret from them. It felt good to be honest, but I wasn't ready to share who might be back in town.

"We were on our way to Huntsville to meet with a prisoner when Flores got the call."

Amelia set her glass down a bit too hard. "Wait. What? What was Flores thinking taking you to such a horrible place? I can't imagine what that would be like."

I smiled at her protectiveness. At least I knew someone cared. "No, it was fine. I wanted to go. Something about that case brought out a desperation in Flores I found so out of character. I wanted to help."

Gina emptied the bottle into her glass. "What about Rob? What happened?" She swallowed heavily. "Did you see him?"

"No," I said. "Flores went to the scene, and I ubered home." To keep my hands busy before I drank the next bottle by myself, I moved the food to the already set table while Amelia sliced the skirt steak.

Gina slumped into her dining room seat, already twisting the top off the second—third for me—wine bottle. "I'm sorry, Fauna. I'm just desperate for information, not that it will help anything. We've been so concerned with that horrible illness that's ravishing the homeless population. Rob was working hard to get extra funding for their care and information to keep them safe. I don't know what we're going to do now."

"Illness?" Amelia asked as she joined us with the meat.

"Well, it's like a wasting sickness of some sort. Like something saps them of all strength." Gina built her first fajita with extra peppers and onions. "Sadly, we can't seem to get much interest from the medical community, since it only seems to affect the homeless."

Maybe there was something I could do. "I could ask Tucker about it. He must have seen something as an ER doc."

Amelia pulled the Cholula from the fridge before taking her seat. "How is that hunk of hotness doing? We haven't seen him lately."

That was a good question. He wasn't into the club scene as much as I was; it was foreplay for me. He didn't know I was an empath or how hard it was for me to open up in an intimate way unless my liver was swimming. I sensed he wanted more, and I didn't know if I had more to give. "He's been super busy with work."

This time Amelia and Gina exchanged worried glances.

"All right, you two. Don't read too much into this."

Gina's phone buzzed, and she glanced at the screen. Her fajita fell out of her hand, and she gasped. The sharp tang of surprise rippled from Gina. I closed my eyes and sang my mother's hymn so I didn't dive deep into her emotions. I had to get it under control, because it was too hard to be supportive when I was just as overwhelmed as she was. I'd used my mother's singing voice since I was a teenager, but the Collected had taught me how to make it more effective.

After blocking the external emotions that were only slightly numbed by the wine, I opened my eyes to Amelia reading what looked like a group chat on Gina's phone.

She whistled and poured more wine into Gina's cup. "I'm so sorry." She highlighted one word and held up the screen to me: *suicide*.

Relief washed over me. "So not murder then." I immediately regretted the words. Though I was selfishly grateful I'd taken a moment to protect my own psyche, for Gina burst into tears.

Amelia gave me a weary look as she moved behind Gina and hugged her over the back of the chair.

"I'm sorry, Gina." I couldn't tell her that the familiar mob of emotions at the scene had developed into a fear of what it meant. A self-inflicted event meant whether what I had felt was fresh or old, he had nothing to do with it. But Gina's emotions were as far from relief as you could get.

Gina shook her head as much as she could with Amelia comforting her. "It can't be suicide. Rob was always happy and always entertaining the volunteers with his humor. There's no way he could have taken his own life while his people, as he called them, were still suffering. He just wouldn't."

My intimate experience with outer versus inner emotions had taught me that many extremely depressed people used humor and plastered on smiles to hide what they truly suffered. "I could ask Flores if he can share anything."

Gina's head popped up. "Oh, could you? I mean, it can't be right."

As Amelia took back her seat, I put my hand over Gina's. "Of course I can."

Her smile made me so grateful I was able to touch her now without being so overwhelmed with her emotions that I couldn't function. I have found my empathic abilities to be much more of a blessing instead of a curse now that I could control when it affected me and when it didn't. Most of the time anyway.

Gina pulled a green pepper from her fajita and nibbled on it. "I really shouldn't have drank all that wine before I ate anything."

Amelia shrugged. "That *is* normally Fauna's MO."

"Hey!" I tossed my napkin at her.

Gina laughed, tickling my toes with her change in mood. I wished I could take away her pain, not just sense it. "So what are y'all up to this week?"

With a side-eyed glance at me, Amelia said, "Well, I have that tech conference at the George R. Brown. And I have an extra badge if someone else wants to come with me."

"Oh no." I waved both hands in front of me as if that would stop her. She'd been trying to get me to go to this conference for years.

Gina held her hand up. "You just touched me with your bare skin and didn't even flinch. And believe me, I'm feeling some things."

Dammit, I might have come a long way in the past few months, but there was no way I was ready for a crowded event with a bunch of strangers. "I opened a little computer repair shop for a reason: way less people."

Amelia slapped a plastic badge on a bright green lanyard next to my plate. "And I've seen your books. If you want to keep that place afloat, you're going to need some corporate work. So many companies are outsourcing their help desks, and you speak English okay."

I had nothing left to toss at her.

"Besides, Chipped is closed on Mondays. You might as well come and hang with me tomorrow." She raised an eyebrow. "I'll even buy lunch at Rustic."

Gina perked up. "Well now I want to go."

I flipped the badge over to reveal the bright yellow logo of the Bayou City IT Summit. "I suppose I could try." I made sure Amelia looked straight at me. "But if the testosterone overwhelms me, I'm out."

"Fair." Amelia dug into her second fajita. I could feel how proud of herself she was.

I wondered how long she'd been planning this ambush.

Chapter Four

Early Monday morning—though not stupid early like when Flores picked me up the day before—Amelia honked her horn outside my townhouse. Before slipping the badge over my head, I smoothed the pencil skirt I dragged from the back of my closet. I had to admit, I was pretty damn proud the old thing still fit. I hadn't worn it in years, not since college graduation. My shoes, though, weren't the high-heeled, sexy things I preferred. My scarred foot wouldn't let me stretch like that anymore. Wedges were the best I could do.

But it was all fine. Today began the new me where I could go out in a crowded venue and not freak the fuck out. At least that was the plan. After grabbing my laptop bag, I headed to Amelia before she could honk again. After the mess last summer, I didn't need my neighbors filing another complaint.

Slipping in the passenger side, I growled at Amelia. "You could text that you're here, you know."

"This way is much more effective." Amelia had straightened her hair, giving it an extra four inches in length. She looked like Uma Thurman in *Kill Bill* but with auburn hair. She was just as much of a badass too. I hadn't seen her up against her mostly male colleagues in a while. It would be fun to see her in her element.

My bag shifted at my feet as she maneuvered around traffic. My eye twitched with my own nervousness; I sensed nothing but confidence radiating from Amelia. To hide my obvious discomfort, I checked to make sure I'd packed my Chipped business cards. Just like the first seven times, they were tucked nicely in the little pocket designed for them. I'd never even used the cards. Half of them I threw away before finding enough undamaged ones to hand out without shame.

"You're doing it again." Amelia's comment caught me off guard.

"Doing what?"

She sighed. "You can literally sense other's emotions, yet you're not very in tune with your own."

"Ah." Ever since I'd confessed my abilities to my BFFs, they'd expected me to open up constantly about what I was going through. It wasn't that simple. A lifetime of hiding who I really was made it difficult to break free from those self-imposed restraints, even for those who loved me dearly. "I'm sorry. I did my meditation to prepare for today, but I think I need to center again before going in. My mind kept wandering with all the what-if scenarios."

"You'll be fine." She pulled a flask from her bag and shook it enticingly without taking her eyes from the road. "I brought emergency backup, just in case."

"I love you." And I did. I really did. "But I'm going to do this without numbing alcohol." If I said it loud enough, I might even believe it myself.

Amelia tried to hide her skeptical look, but she needn't bother. My stomach rolled with indigestion while my gut cramped at the same time. It was a unique feeling tied to lying, like a combination of guilt and fear. That unique sensation was why I could usually tell when people lied. Though I was pretty sure I was feeling my own lack of truth instead of Amelia's.

So I confessed my true intention. "At least until lunch. I'm not eating at Rustic without a drink."

We chitchatted for the rest of the drive, which proved a lot shorter than I expected. Panic fought within me as Amelia pulled into the underground parking garage. Attendees seemed to pour from cars and multiply at the elevators and on the exit ramps.

Amelia frowned when we passed an obnoxiously red Porsche SUV. "Of all the people I didn't want to see today." She pulled into a parking spot four cars down.

I probably should have asked her to elaborate, but I was too busy panicking. My seatbelt didn't want to obey my shaking hands and release. I left my gloves in my bag because I could totally handle this. The Collected showed me how. But now that I sat here and the air rolled with all these other people, I knew I'd gone too far too fast. I needed to start somewhere less crowded—like Disney World.

Amelia placed a calming hand on my shoulder. She had no idea how much that truly helped. "I know you can do this."

A man walked behind the car and my guts tightened almost painfully. He was really mad about something. Okay, maybe I wasn't ready for this at all. I thought I could handle the emotions, but if my body itself refused to separate, I was in deep trouble. If I couldn't even block out the emotions in the air, how was I supposed to stay sane if I shook a hand? This was, after all, a networking event. No one would hire a consultant who shook their hand wearing gloves. Of course, I was getting ahead of myself. If I couldn't get out of the car, there would be no handshaking.

I breathed in slowly, filling my lungs to capacity. After counting to five, I pushed the air out through my mouth. The tightness of my diaphragm reverberated through my muscles, aggravating the scars in my recently healed body. Oddly, that gave me strength. If I could survive a serial killer, if I could recover from the devastating injuries he caused, then I could face a bunch of tech pros at a business convention.

My gut loosened as I drove away the sensation using sheer willpower. "Give me five minutes to center and I'll be good to go."

Amelia leaned back in her chair and sipped her coffee, giving me time. I really did love her. I cued up Mom's hymn. Once she was nice and strong, I explored my own emotions and placed each of them in the front of my mind. I'd never realized that by protecting myself from other people's emotions, I'd also been suppressing my own. Turned out, if I had a strong idea of what I was feeling, it was easier to separate myself from those around me. Though I wanted to avoid the nervousness, I couldn't deny its presence. Hopefully, it would fade when I started talking to people. There was also a hefty dose of excitement. As much as Amelia had to force me to come, I was looking forward to talking to others in the field. And she was right, a few corporate clients would loosen the financial stress of running such a small business. Lastly, I rolled the University of Houston class ring around my middle finger. Hopefully it would help me sway some business to my side, and it was what I chose as my centering vehicle for when I lost my mind. Because it would happen.

With Mom's voice in the background and my own mixed emotions in the foreground, I was ready. It was phenomenal how much better I functioned when I could at least protect myself from the physical reactions of my empathic abilities. I was gorgeously relaxed at this point. I felt like an autonomous person, which was super rare for me. I could get used to this. Before I opened my eyes, I took one more breath in and out.

That must have cued Amelia, for she popped her door open and grabbed her laptop bag from the back seat. "Let's go. I want to grab another cup of coffee before the line is out the door."

Without even flinching when an SUV parked right next to us and the passengers piled out, I pulled myself from the car. A bit of energy floated in the air around the group, but my body didn't react to anything they were feeling.

Is this what normal people felt? The uncursed? A smile lifted my lips and lightened my step as Amelia kept pace beside me.

When we got to the entrance of the George R. Brown Convention Center, Amelia nodded at me like a coach before the big game. "Here we go."

On the other side of the bank of red doors with large circular windows, a gasp escaped before I could stop it at the crowd of milling business-clothed professionals. The chatting—not animatedly, it was still early—group stood in a mostly orderly line waiting to get into the hall. My centering held steady as a wave of mixed emotion didn't touch me at all. As we found the end of the line, I could sense a bit of the gentleman in front of me. Ants seemed to crawl over my scalp. Some of it might have been my own nerves, but a bit definitely emanated from the middle-aged man in the navy-blue polo and khakis. For some reason, it actually made me feel better. He blended in at this event like one more piece in a rather uniform puzzle and he was nervous. I'd be fine.

"Larry?" Amelia's upturned voice came from behind me.

The polo-clad white guy turned around. His face lifted and back straightened. "Amelia McLauren, as I live and breathe."

I got a whiff of his leathery aftershave and a tickle in my toes as his worry morphed to happiness. Something about his general aura was familiar.

Amelia raised an eyebrow at me. So sweet of her to ask if I was ready, but then dive into the introductions without awaiting my response. "Fauna, meet Larry Wellers. He runs the internal and external help desk for Techs 'R' Us." She smiled sweetly to the older man. "And this, Larry, is my best friend Fauna Young who owns her own computer repair shop called Chipped."

Larry held out his hand. "Nice to meet you, Fauna."

Okay. This was it. The moment of truth. With only a tiny crack in my voice, I responded in kind, "Nice to meet you too."

His fingers tucked under my wrist in a warm, cushiony shake. He didn't try to break my hand, and I sensed nothing beyond a tightening in the pit of my stomach. To my relief, I realized it was my own fear, not his.

My face warmed as I released his hand and my tensed jaw. A raised eyebrow and tilted upper lip at Amelia communicated all I felt tied into one action. I could totally do this.

Amelia winked, before turning back to Larry. "What brings you out to the Summit. I thought you were past this sort of hobnobbing."

He shrugged, reminding me of Jeff, my one employee. "The CIO wants us represented just in case Framework shows up. He doesn't really think they're a threat, but if they look like they're making a move on some of our clients, I'm supposed to call him immediately."

"Ah," I felt so good I was ready to join the conversation, "so you're here as a spy. Sneaky."

Larry sucked in his stomach and adjusted his belt. "Double O Nerd. Wellers, Larry Wellers."

Amelia shook her head like she did at Gina and I when we were being silly. "I'm pretty sure I saw Omar's car in the parking garage. It's probably wise you came out."

Larry groaned. "Not that obnoxious, cherry-red Porsche SUV."

"With the ridiculous black leather interior. Makes no sense for the Houston summer." Amelia moved us forward as the line progressed. "I got a ride in that thing once. Burned my calves even with the seat coolers on."

"It has seat coolers?" Look at me having a casual conversation while surrounded by a crowd of strangers. The hum I felt right now was with my ears, not my every nerve. It was refreshing.

"Yep." Amelia nodded. "They kind of suck air through these little vents in the seats."

Larry seemed to catch up to the conversation. "You rode in his car?"

No shame dripped from Amelia's tilted head. "He made me a job offer and took me to lunch in that obnoxious thing. That was when I knew I couldn't work for him. I mean, if you're going to buy an SUV as a single man, Landrover all the way, baby."

The main doors must have opened because the line started to move at a good pace. When we crossed the threshold after the bored-looking attendants glanced at our badges, Larry waved at us.

"I better go catch a live sighting, then call the boss. I don't want to have to ride in that Porsche to get a new job."

"Smart move." Amelia laughed.

I waved. "It was nice meeting you, Larry."

"And you, Fauna." He pointed at me as he walked backward. "I might be calling you. I could use a dependable hardware guy."

"Wait." I remembered my cards and handed him one. "Take one. I'd love to give it a go."

He tucked it in the pocket of his badge. "You bet."

Chapter Five

Amelia and I perused a couple booths. We ran into a few people from our UofH days but mostly strangers. Most of the activity was a blur as I hopped around on cloud nine, ecstatic I didn't feel attacked on all sides, *and* I was sober. That was definitely a first.

I might have even made a few promising contacts. How had I let my empathic abilities keep me from all of this possibility for so long? A bit of discipline and some strong friends by my side made all the difference.

Everything flowed pretty smoothly until Amelia grabbed my elbow and turned her back on a crowded booth decked out with instruction manuals for all sorts of computer languages. With a head tilt, she indicated a loud-talking man in his forties with a full head of dark hair and a trim waist. He could be considered good-looking, but judging by the grimace on Amelia's face, that wasn't why she wanted me to notice him.

"That's Bob," she said through clenched teeth.

I was missing something. "And that means ...?" The back of my neck burned from Amelia's loathing. The morning of blocking as much as I could had worn me out; her strong emotion busted through a bit too easily. I twisted my class ring to recenter.

"That's my boss, Bob. I thought he wasn't going to make it to this, so many important emails to write or something equally dire kept him away. Or so he said."

Her loathing suddenly made sense. "Oh, that Bob, the one who always steals your ideas and gives you no credit."

Her tense smile and slight nod affirmed my assertion. I was having trouble keeping her out of my head with the direct touch, but I didn't want to snatch my arm away. She obviously needed the contact. If only I could calm her the way she usually did me. As the smug man leaned over the counter to flirt with the booth babes hocking some new app to reduce all those tech manuals to a Duolingo model for computer programming, I thought maybe I could do some good here.

I winked at Amelia. "I think I need to meet him."

My burning neck morphed to a bit of tingling as Amelia switched from loathing to anxiety before her hand fell away. "No, please, I was having a great day, and I don't want to fuck it up with Bob."

"It's time for you to trust me. I can help." Ignoring my friend's pleas, I removed her hand from my arm. Amelia had protected me for years. It was time to return the favor. With the way Bob leered at the women trying to make a sale, I had a feeling I could discover some sort of leverage for her to use. Time to take her power back.

After a slight hesitation, Amelia mirrored my straight-backed march. "Bob?" she called when we were close enough to be seen through the crowd.

He turned the bottom half of his body first as if taking his eyes off the young girls was just too painful to contemplate. His face lit up when he picked Amelia from the crowd. He apparently didn't realize how she felt about him at all. Sometimes, I wished everyone had a bit of empathic ability. How nice would it be if everyone understood more readily what someone else felt?

His voice surprised me more than his put-together appearance. Its deep resonance evoked a strong, confident man, not one who leered at women and took their ideas. "Amelia, I'm so glad we ran into each other." His eyes scanned my entire physique before resting on my face. "Who's your friend?"

In a club, I expected—even demanded—that I get looked at like that. It was kind of the point. In this professional setting, it gave me the creeps.

Though her eyebrows crinkled, Amelia introduced us. "Bob, this is my friend Fauna Young. We went to school together."

After doing my best to stifle a shutter, I held my hand out in greeting.

He accepted it as if he humored a child at play. "It's a pleasure to meet you, Fauna."

I had to resist the urge to punch him, especially since I needed to suppress as much of me as possible so I could do a clean reading. Luckily, he seemed eager to continue holding my hand since I needed time to interpret his state of mind. Though my breasts tingled with his obvious attraction, his lust seemed dulled, like it was superficial. Underneath all the swagger and coiffed appearance lay an emptiness that made my chest feel concave, for a moment I couldn't breathe.

Interesting. This man had zero confidence whatsoever. No wonder he always claimed Amelia's ideas as his. He had to cover for his own lack of ability. Though I'm not sure what sort of advantage this revelation would give Amelia.

Just as I was going to start the interrogation to see what else I could discover, Bob's anxiety spiked causing my head to itch so bad I had to pull my hand back to make it stop. Not my favorite emotion to sense. It always made me feel like I had lice or something.

A voice thick with the confidence Bob lacked coated the back of my neck. "Amelia, is that you?"

Amelia widened her eyes at me as she answered, "Yes, Omar. I'm still not interested in working for Framework."

So the infamous Omar. I turned and cocked my hip in friend solidarity against the creep. But when I actually saw him, I almost tripped in my sensible shoes. The man belonged on a big screen with his high cheekbones, strong jaw, deep brown eyes, almost black hair, and burnished skin that sparkled like honey. How in the hell had Amelia said no to anything Omar asked? She was a much stronger woman than I.

As I ogled this god of a man, I realized I was being just as creepy as Bob had been. *Come on, Fauna. You're better than that. Save it for the club.* Which naturally led me to wonder where Omar got his dance on.

"And, Bob, the boss I couldn't pry you away from." He winked at Bob, and I sensed Bob's nervousness spike even though I no longer touched him.

Well, that was interesting. What did it mean?

Bob cleared his throat and made a familiar up nod of his head. His feet shuffled like he was ready to be somewhere else.

Amelia hadn't taken her focus from Omar. She stood with her hip cocked and her arms crossed. "Are you here to actually sell your services and check in on clients or are you here to poach people?"

"Maybe a little of both." His gaze focused on me. "If no one's going to introduce us, I'll have to do the honors. I'm Omar Damini, owner of Framework."

To his credit, he kept his eyes on my face as he extended his hand. Now I felt even more guilty about my reaction when I first saw him. He might have been a business shark, but so far seemed like a perfect gentleman. I guess I'd find out soon enough.

As our hands touched, lust did not permeate. Instead, my fingers tingled and my gut tightened slightly like it would if I was trying to balance myself. So he was curious. About what? Me?

"I'm Fauna Young." The mention of my name did not dull the curiosity.

"Do you work with Bob too? I mean, for now."

Amelia scoffed. "Seriously?"

While she chewed him out, only amusement drifted from his hand into me. "Spoilers?"

When I drew back from our handshake, Bob bumped past me. The subtle tap sent a wave of nausea through me followed by an intense gut cramp. The man swam with guilt and fear, neither of which he felt before Omar got there.

Bob gestured toward the exit. "Uh, Omar, don't we have that lunch meet-and-greet to get to."

Teeth just crooked enough to add character peeked out of Omar's wide grin. "Of course, Bob employee of Stratagem. We should probably get going, or we'll be late."

Amelia stepped up to me and shook her head. "What in the heck was that?"

The cramping in my gut subsided as Bob moved away with Omar. "I don't know exactly, but …" Considering the lack of confidence, then the fear and guilt when he saw Omar and Omar's hints at poaching employees. Holy shit. "I take that back I do know."

"Well, don't leave me hanging."

"Omar hired Bob. He's leaving Stratagem."

Amelia's jaw opened so wide, I had to resist closing it. "But bonuses won't be cut for another month. If the big wigs find out."

"That explains why he was so afraid. He must be waiting for the check to clear before putting in his notice."

Amelia guided me to one of the bold red exit doors. "Which means his job will need filling and I could use this info to encourage him to give me a huge recommendation."

"Yep. You could probably even convince him to give you credit for that code you wrote last year that he called a 'team effort' so the 'team lead' would get the extra kudos."

"Fauna, you're a genius."

Though my head throbbed and different parts of my body continuously rebelled as I got too close to one person than another on the crowded sidewalk, I pulled my own pride to the forefront to try and soak it up. *Yes, what I did was probably unethical, but I did it for a friend, not my own self-interest. That made it okay, right?*

The Rustic's large wooden fence seemed out of place amongst the cement and glass of the big city. Its good-ole-boy charm mixed with the elevated food and fancy cocktails was exactly what I needed right now. "Let's stuff our face and make plans to take over the world."

Amelia slipped her arm into my cocked elbow. "And I'm buying."

Chapter Six

The street looked completely different after a hearty meal of smoked brisket tacos and wood-grilled broccolini. The more than two Palomas did a grand job of numbing my sensitivities. But I wasn't sure I was ready to hit that floor again. "Do we have to tour more booths?"

Amelia pressed the crosswalk button leading back to the GRB. "Definitely not. It's time to go to a few panels. There's one about integrating mobile gaming with blockchain I've been curious about."

I leaned against the metal pole to give her that look. "Boring integrated with super boring."

"Well, if you want excitement, we could hit the bar at the hotel and see who shows up." Amelia offered, and I was pretty sure she was only partially joking.

Though tempting, I wasn't sure if I was fully up to crowded, emotionally heavy spots for the rest of the day. "We should probably head to the deluxe boredom of the panel. Hopefully, everyone will be sleepy after lunch making their emotional reactions dull. I could handle a little dull."

The light turned, and Amelia flourished her arms as if inviting royalty to go first. So I did. As I skipped up to the curve on the other side, like a proper princess, my foot gave out and twisted. Seriously? I hadn't consumed *that* much alcohol. To stop from collapsing totally in the street, I grabbed the young tree in the breath of greenery in the cement walkway.

Then it happened again. That same feeling of familiarity, like I'd forgotten something and the back of my mind tried to remind me, flowed from the tree. It was identical to the one I felt at St. Benedict's yesterday. The Palomas had my senses numb, but it also made it difficult to maintain my new barriers. How long could an impression last? I didn't even know if I should call this an impression. There was no memory attached, no falling into someone else's mind, just a ghost of an aura of someone I used to be close to, a ghost from my past, that should not have been there.

"Watch it," Amelia cautioned as she caught me before I face planted into the cement. "Are you okay?"

Her worry mixed with my fear sobered me up quickly. "I'm fine." I was not fine, but what could I do about it?

Amelia's worry changed to joy that tickled at my fingertips. "Is that Austin?"

Blinking to clear the dark from my thoughts, I followed her look to the corner heading behind the GRB under 59. The young man in the skinny jeans, stylish untucked button-up, and confident swagger was definitely Flores's husband Austin. I wondered why he was down here.

"Austin!" Amelia yelled, her voice barely carrying over the noise of the traffic overhead.

His shoulders caved in before he turned around slowly. Was he afraid of being seen? I swore to whatever goddess had the power, if Austin was cheating on Flores, I'd make him pay. When his search found us, he smiled gently and seemed to relax. Not exactly the stance of a caught cheater.

"Heya, girls. What're y'all doing down here?" He brushed aside his blonde bangs as the wind blew them over his eyes. Austin was such a pretty man; I teased Flores that he bagged a trophy husband. Austin loved the term so much, he started using it when he introduced the two. "Where's Gina?"

"It's a school day. She's at work." Amelia motioned to the polo-clad crew filing back into the George R. Brown. "Fauna and I are here for the Bayou City IT Seminar. You're not looking for clients amongst the geekdom, are you?"

Austin was a talented and in-demand interior designer. As we got within talking instead of shouting distance, my eye twitched picking up on his nervousness. What was he trying to hide?

With a shaky laugh, Austin looked over his shoulder before answering. "No, I'm actually ... Well, you see, I'm down here to meet someone." When both mine and Amelia's eyes grew three times their size, Austin shook his hands to wave off the accusations obvious in our expressions. "No, no, no, it's not like that. This is for Mateo."

It was my turn to nervously laugh. "He sends you downtown to meet guys for him? That's so modern of you."

"No, not ... I have to help him, but he can't know I'm here." He leaned in and grabbed my ungloved hands before I could back up.

Unprepared for the sudden contact, my chest burned like it was on fire. On top of that, my eyes grew heavy from a sharp pain in the back of them. His guilt and sadness threatened to overwhelm any sort of clear thinking I possessed. "What did you do?"

Amelia pushed Austin off me and stepped in between us, reprising her role as my protector. I was too grateful for the cessation of the physical reaction to be annoyed. Though her worry made my already hurting eyes twitch. As more businesspeople headed by us on their way back to the convention, I was struck by wave after wave of varying emotions from satisfaction to happiness to anxiety to fear. The rawness of the onslaught and my inability to shut them out reminded me why I didn't come to these things.

My hands wrapped around my center as if their squeeze

could prevent my rapidly beating heart from bursting out of my chest. Tension caused the scar in my shoulder to pull the muscles in my back as different parts of my body tingled or cramped depending on the whim of emotion from any passerby. I sprinted under the bridge and across the street, away from the mass of the crowd and toward an overgrown lot.

A pleasant warmth eased my panic as Amelia came up behind me. Between her closeness and the crowd's distance, her love and concern overpowered any random emotion from a stranger. I clung to that sensation until everything else faded to a bad memory. She handed me her liquor flask without judgement, and I took a generous swig without guilt. The sharp burn down my throat contrasted with the comforting heat from Amelia. After a few minutes of Amelia standing guard and Austin pacing like a cornered rabbit, the lemon-flavored vodka kicked in and numbed my empathic abilities enough that I had room for my own emotions again.

And what did I feel? Anger. Without warning, I turned on Austin. "All right, enough avoiding our questions. Out with it or I call Flores right now."

Austin's chiseled cheeks glistened with tears. "Don't call him, please. Not yet anyway. I need to see if she's real first."

She? Well, he definitely wasn't cheating then.

Still defensively between me and Austin, Amelia crossed her arms. "What are you talking about?"

As if someone breached the dam, words flooded from Austin's mouth. "There's a healer in town. Mateo thinks it's bullshit, but his cousin is dying and it's eating him up inside and I want to help him. I've heard so much about this healer and what she can do. It's all over the paranormal blog I follow. She's traveled through Texas and finally made it to Houston, and I just have to see her. If I can prove she's real to Flores, then maybe he'll take her to see his cousin and she'll heal him and then I can have my Mateo back."

My mind swirled with Austin's explanation. "He was pretty stressed on Sunday and even less talkative than normal."

How had I missed how personal Flores's stress was? I'd thought he was worried about the case and guilty that he'd caught the wrong guy. I suppose the intensity I sensed made more sense if he was bogged down with a family tragedy in the making as well. "But there's no such thing as a healer. Maybe we can call Tucker and see if he knows a specialist or something?"

Amelia's face tightened, and her arms fell to her side. "That makes more sense to me. Let us help you, Austin."

His handsome face paled under his bottle tan. "I can't believe you two. Knowing what Fauna can do, why can't you believe there are other things out there that are real but can't be explained."

My mouth fell open as Amelia and I exchanged a shocked look. I didn't even bother to deny his accusation. "How do you—"

"You and Mateo might think you're whispering, but I have excellent hearing. I've watched from upstairs as you touch things and give him readings." With newfound confidence, Austin marched around us heading toward a parking lot in desperate need of repairs.

I rushed to keep up, with Amelia on my heels. "Readings are a con. I share memories that might be left on the evidence he brings me."

He abruptly stopped and pivoted to face us both. "Why does he believe you, someone he rescued last year from a murderer, instead of his own husband who has been following the paranormal world for years. Humans can do all kinds of things, but he can't seem to believe anything unless he sees it for himself."

I had to slide to a stop to avoid running into him. My ankle protested, but I didn't stumble this time. "Maybe that's because of his training. Just because I and a couple of others are empaths doesn't mean magic is real or whatever. We're just wired differently."

He walked around a group of people and right into the parking lot where more people than I'd expect were milling about. "I didn't say anything about magic. Though if you don't think whatever you do is magic, I don't know what to call it. If you can be a true empath, then there could also be a true healer."

Truthfully, I had no idea why the Collected had these abilities. Maybe he was right. Not too long ago, I thought I was the only empath in the world. But I couldn't let him get conned. I more than most knew the real possibility of that outcome. "Okay, fair. How about you let us come with you and make sure this healer is the real thing?" Not that I had any idea how to do that. Maybe I could call Belinda and have her meet us. Since she could sense empaths, maybe she'd know if this person had other powers.

"Um, Fauna?" Amelia's tone quieted the argument that formed on my tongue. "Maybe we should do this another day, like when you're not so tired."

Her surprise mirrored my own when I realized what I'd just walked into. I'd never been so grateful for the slight drunken haze which was probably the only thing that saved me from the onslaught of god knows what would surround the crowd of mostly homeless people. The entire surface moved like a disrupted anthill. The smell of unwashed people in the Houston heat would have caused me to cross the street on any normal day. On the outskirts, businesspeople and college students and I don't know what else joined the crowd. Even through my numbness, one emotion called out above all others: hope. My body tingled pleasantly, not just my fingers or my toes, but all of me.

I smiled weakly at Amelia. "I think I'll be okay. Whatever is happening here, the crowd is eager and hopeful." And it felt good. I might never leave.

Amelia grabbed Austin's shoulder, stopping him from pushing his way into the crowd. "If that's the stage, we'll see just fine from here."

She nodded toward a raised platform pieced together from

old pallets haphazardly balanced on top of ten-gallon buckets. Directly behind it idled a mid-sized RV. "Whoever decides to stand on that thing might need a healer."

Austin laughed and the joyful sound eased the tension between the three of us. We were family after all, at least the closest I had to it.

The crowd quieted as the side door on the RV popped open. Out stepped a man dressed in jeans and a T-shirt, behind him, a petite woman in a cute sundress in shades of green and cute, blush-colored shoes. Her tan skin glowed in the sun as she mounted the platform with the guidance of her male companion. I had to admit there was something about the way she smiled sweetly at the crowd that made me understand her appeal, but I couldn't tell you if she had any abilities or not.

To hype the crowd, the white male companion jumped on the platform that bounced sketchily, but neither speaker seemed to balk at the instability. As he turned downstage, my skin crawled and I resisted the urge to run and hide. Just a bit too long, his dark hair puffed out around his head in a way that looked haphazard but I knew to be intentional. With eyes the same gray as mine, he scanned the gathered hopefuls, searching for his next victim.

Amelia gasped. "Isn't that—?"

"Yes," I interrupted her. "That's Forrest."

Austin tilted his head. "You know him."

"Unfortunately. You might as well leave, because I guarantee this is all a scam."

His hope wasn't so easy to dismiss. "But how do you know? They haven't done anything yet."

"Oh, he's done plenty." At least I knew what I'd sensed in the street and the homeless shelter was real, and it wasn't old at all. "He's my brother."

Chapter Seven

It had been so long, and Forrest promised never to return to Houston. I didn't know why I believed him even for a second. One happy side effect had my anger peaked so high it easily drowned out the eagerness of the crowd. Regardless of what Austin believed, humans couldn't do the miraculous things he imagined. Which was a good thing for Forrest at this moment, because if I had the power of telekinesis, I'd knock him right off that platform and into oncoming traffic.

Oh dear god, what am I thinking? He was my brother, even after everything he did. He might be toxic to me and those he was around, but he didn't deserve death. And I didn't deserve to turn myself into a murderer. Yet, I couldn't let him take more victims with his current scheme. Not after last time, the final con I pulled with him. I'd first have to figure out how he was doing it this time. If I exposed him, Forrest would have to leave with his tail between his legs, and I could go back to my steady, mostly uneventful life.

Amelia glared at my brother. She didn't even know what we did, but she knew he hurt me. Badly.

I elbowed her and gestured to the stage. "I need to get a little closer." Plus, I felt exposed on the outskirts, like somehow his gaze would find me. I'd never get a straight answer then. If I was mixed into the crowd, I could use them as camouflage. I took my gloves from my shoulder bag and pulled them on as high as they would go.

"All right. If you're sure." Amelia cut through the crowd with confidence as I surfed in her wake. Austin brought up the rear. "But when we're finished here, I expect a full explanation. You never shared with Gina and I why you broke all contact with your brother."

"Now that you know everything about me, I suppose there's nothing left to hide." But there was. There was a lot more.

Nevertheless, Amelia seemed satisfied for the moment. I guessed we'd get into it later.

I put a hand on Amelia's shoulder to use her determination and my seething anger to act as a barrier to the crashing wave of emotion from hope to desperation that swirled around me. I was definitely going to need more practice at honing my protections if I was going to continue to find myself in crowds. Amelia lead us to stage right, far enough back to blend in with a curious lunch crowd but not too far back that we couldn't see everything that was happening on the makeshift stage.

Forrest's voice carried, like it always had. He had an engaging presence. That was why he was such a good con artist. "Thank you for coming this afternoon. We won't be long in Houston, but we wanted to do as much good while we were passing through as we could."

"We love you, man!" yelled a guy with a Spanish accent in the back, his clothes two sizes too big.

The crowd echoed the same sentiment in different languages and different words, but the emotion seemed to add up to a tidal wave of love that heated my blood. Their enthusiasm morphed to more of an obsession. It had to be from the overwhelming amount of donors. I found myself enthralled. If I didn't have personal experience with Forrest to combat the worship, I just might have fallen in line with the rest.

Amelia pushed back an older woman who mumbled to herself without looking in any direction in particular. "Are you sure you're okay?"

"I'm definitely not okay. But I have to see for myself."

She held her hands up in acquiescence but scanned the crowd like a secret service agent. I didn't deserve her.

"We love you too." Forrest waited for the murmurs to die down. "It is my great honor to introduce Heidi, the Healer."

If I thought the crowd was passionate before, the new level of cheering and intense joy washed away any anger still simmering inside. Shouts of greeting escaped my lips before I knew I was going to do it. "Heidi, the Healer!"

"See!" Austin clapped and whistled. "She's the real thing."

Amelia raised an eyebrow at me but scoffed at Austin. "She hasn't done anything yet."

He pointed at Amelia running his gaze from head to foot. "You need a bit more belief in your life."

Amelia wasn't bothered by him at all. "And you need a bit more logic."

Despite myself, I enjoyed the ebb and flow of hope and happiness in the crowd. It was like being at the club without all the lust. Then Forrest spoke again and toppled me off my high. I had to focus, or I'd miss the trick.

"Heidi, as many of you know, has been gifted with a special ability. It is not limitless, however."

Murmuring rippled through the crowd. He was losing them. Also, it was interesting that he ran a scam that had limits. Of course, I'd never seen any sort of spiritual healing where the whole group was made well. Apparently, this was just part of the game.

Forrest's gaze roamed over the heads of the crowd as if he searched for someone in particular. When he shifted our way, I looked straight down. My hair was a different color and I'd put on a few pounds from the last time we'd seen each other. If I was lucky, he'd skim right over me.

Whatever he was searching for, I couldn't discern. He pulled Heidi forward and pointed her to stage left. "Heidi will ask her gift to find a recipient. Now you must close your eyes and call out in your minds for recognition and the gift will choose the most desperate and most deserving among you. For we are mere mortals and have no right to choose who is healed and who must continue to suffer. We must put our faith in the gift."

The mix of people who would pass each other on the street without making eye contact acted as one and bowed their heads, like paying homage at a prayer meeting. Oh, I didn't like this one bit. Forrest was bad enough when he was conning people out of money by "speaking" to their missing or dead loved ones. I couldn't imagine what depths he would sink to protect this pull he had over these people.

From my downward angle, I couldn't see much except for Forrest directing Heidi. Of course, he had a pre-selected person. Whether the sick person was a plant or paid Forrest for the service, my conniving brother certainly wouldn't leave this bit to chance.

His voice—the one that had once comforted me in the night when the memories that weren't my own haunted me—rang out, awakening the audience from its silence. "The gift has chosen. Heidi?"

Murmurs floated above the crowd like the hope that was soon to turn to disappointment for most of them. I folded my arms and cued up Mom's hymn to try and protect me from the abrupt change. I didn't have the fortitude to call up any of the new techniques without fully grounding myself. Maybe I shouldn't have drank so much.

Heidi's petite frame looked shaky next to Forrest's firm stance. She pointed to a well-dressed woman in a wheelchair, pushed by someone who looked like her servant rather than her adult child. So, it was a paying client.

"Please come forward. The gift has chosen you." The way Heidi stumbled over the word "gift" made me think she wasn't as on board with the healing for money bit as Forrest was.

Amelia whispered, "Is that Michelle?"

I'd been concentrating so hard on trying to pick up something, anything, from Heidi I hadn't paid much attention to the woman who pushed aside people so the old lady could roll to the front of the stage. Though she'd dyed her hair bright blue, I'd recognize her scowl through the fake smile anywhere.

"That's definitely Michelle. I can't believe she's still with him."

Austin leaned between us. "Who's Michelle?"

"See the woman with blue hair just in front of the lady in the wheelchair?" I indicated the second ghost from my past. "When Forrest and I, well, when we used to con people," I swiped my elbow to push away the shock from Austin, "Michelle acted as our liaison: setting up meetings, doing research beforehand, even acting as a fake client if we drew a crowd. She had a gift for blending in and doing whatever Forrest needed her to do."

Amelia sniffed. "Pretty sure she was in love with him."

"Are you sure you're not the empath?" I laughed, then covered my mouth quickly, as the man in front of me, who smelled like he hadn't bathed in days, glared at me. I cleared my throat and focused on Amelia to prevent my gut from tensing. "She was definitely in love with him. But he never even noticed her as a woman."

Austin sighed. "Well, now I feel bad for her. It's awful that she's still clinging to him. Maybe he noticed her later?"

Judging by the way Forrest fawned over Heidi, I doubted it. "One can hope."

Heidi sat on the edge of the stage with her legs swinging over the warped wood of a pallet. "What is your name?" she asked the old lady.

I was glad we'd moved into the crowd. We couldn't have heard her all the way in the back. The audience seemed to want to hear everything the Healer said as well, for they all quieted their movement to try and pick up every sound. The anticipation ran through my system, speeding up my heart rate. I didn't know how much was me and how much was them.

"Jasmina," her voice sounded stronger than her body seemed capable of.

"May I have your hand, Jasmina?" Heidi held hers out.

Jasmina seemed to call on a great effort to raise her arm and place a limp hand inside Heidi's.

After placing her other hand on top of the weak one, Heidi closed her eyes. "Your nerves betray you. You should have many more years, but your quality of life suffers greatly." She opened her eyes, and I was struck by the luminescent blue.

Tears streamed down Jasmina's face. All she managed was a nod in reply.

Forrest interrupted Heidi's quiet time with her patient as he called to the crowd. "Jasmina has a nervous system disorder. Heidi will heal her now, but we need everyone here to help by closing their eyes and chanting 'healer.'"

He started it off with a gentle clapping to set the tempo and the crowd followed suit, like a carefully choreographed number. Austin bowed his head in sync with the others. Amelia shrugged and played along. I closed my eyes as well but tried to focus on Heidi through the distractions. How could she work like this? I needed everything else blocked so I could concentrate on my target.

Then I realized how much easier it was to block the bystanders when they were all chanting in unison with the same intensions. I was able to easily knock them from my senses as one group instead of isolating each individual and moving on to the next. Even Amelia, whom I knew well and stood right beside me, was easy to brush aside from my own psyche as she chanted with the others.

THE HEALER

After centering myself in a way I never imagined possible, I opened my eyes to watch Heidi. She'd jumped off the stage and kneeled before the wheelchair. With both of the ill woman's hands grasped against her chest, Heidi focused her bright blue eyes on Jasmina. With the noise barrier, I found it much easier to isolate Heidi from the others present. I found myself creeping closer to her. As if they sensed me and moved aside, the crowd parted before me.

I moved until I had a perfect line of sight between myself and that wheelchair. Unsure of what I felt, I crept even closer. There was some sort of energy radiating from Heidi. I'd never experienced anything like it. Even the servant who still held the arms of the wheelchair swayed slightly like she was high. I couldn't believe what I was feeling. Heidi wasn't fake. She couldn't be. No one could fake this level of intensity.

At once, something popped. I fell back a step like a string had attached me to Heidi and snapped abruptly. The audience didn't seem to notice a thing for they continued chanting, their speed increasing gently but steadily. Jasmina sighed in her strong voice while Heidi slipped from her grasp and leaned against one of the buckets holding up the pallet stage.

Forrest waved at a reluctant Michelle to help Heidi up. I remembered that attitude. She never wanted to help me either, jealous of my brother's attention. Why had she stuck around to suffer more indifference from my narcissistic brother? How had Michelle not realized the only reason he showed us any attention was to line his pockets and earn the accolades of his customers? Though the large crowd contained more people than the two of us ever managed to accumulate at once. My ability was much more intimate. I couldn't concentrate well enough to read anyone with so many other people's psyches hovering in the background. We specialized in one-on-one encounters for wealthy clients.

Apparently, Forrest had learned a new technique to help Heidi focus. He stomped twice on the stage. Muted by the mass of bodies, the signal only quieted the closest to the stage, but the command circulated through the crowd to the very back.

Weakly, Heidi nodded at Forrest. Was that relief on his face? He had certainly never showed any concern for my well-being. Though they were still in public and that could have been part of the show.

Forrest addressed the crowd again, "Heidi's gift has healed Jasmina."

Amelia spoke behind me to Austin, "That was intense."

The hope in Austin's voice broke my heart. "She's the real thing. I knew she was."

Heidi was certainly real in some way, but it didn't mean she healed anyone. My ability was real too, but I can't talk to the dead or read the signs in the wind to tell the future. There had to be a con here. I just had to figure out what it was.

Forrest turned his attention to the old lady. "How do you feel?"

Jasmina leaned forward. When her servant rushed forward to help her, Jasmina pushed her away. Though shaky, Jasmina managed to balance on her feet.

The servant gasped and tears streamed down her face. "Madam, you stand."

I had to get closer. If I could prove Jasmina was part of the con, I could convince Austin and save Flores from the argument.

One shaky step at a time, Jasmina turned around to face the crowd. "It's a miracle!"

While the crowd and the performers were distracted by the cheering, I got close enough to feel Jasmina's excitement. If I could just touch her, I'd know.

"Fauna?" Michelle's squeaky voice, exactly the same as I remembered it from years ago, stopped me in my tracks.

Panic rose with a flush of warmth in my neck. I tried to back up and stepped on Amelia. Like a new reflex, my hand grasped hers to absorb her quiet confidence to regain my own sense of balance.

Amelia spoke before I could, "Hey, Michelle."

Michelle's eyes narrowed at us.

Oblivious to anything but his money ticket, Forrest guided Heidi around the stage. "Let's hear it for the Healer!"

The crowd roared. I shouted in Amelia's ear. "I have to get out of here now."

Chapter Eight

Without needing to know more, Amelia helped me navigate to the street. We stopped at the outskirts of the crowd. By the time I turned around for one more glance at the stage, Michelle pointed at our fleeing backs. Forrest's focus locked onto mine, and he smiled.

The expression brought back the times when he'd stuff a snack cake in my shirt and guide me out of the convenience store so we'd have something to eat. Or when we both locked Sparrow in the trunk of our car and Forrest sent me to bang on the motel doors one at a time begging for help. When the occupants left to help the little girl with her trapped older brother, Forrest would raid their rooms. After he swiped everything he could, we jumped in the car and took off. One time, we made it all the way to the next motel before we remembered we hadn't let Sparrow out of the trunk. Forrest ran one con after another, but all of it was to take care of us and make sure we ate. With a dead father and a mother who could barely keep her head on straight, our care fell to Forrest because he was the oldest.

My heart melted a little as I fought the urge to go back to the stage. Maybe he had to scam and cheat to keep us alive when we were children, but we weren't children anymore. We had options that didn't involve conning innocent people. I couldn't fall for his charm again.

While Forrest and I stared at each other, Heidi moved to stage right and beckoned to someone in the audience. Forrest tore his focus from me and rushed to Heidi's side. He put both of his hands on her shoulders and pulled her back from the edge. I couldn't hear anything from so far away, but they were obviously arguing. Forrest nodded Michelle to shoo away the young dark-haired girl who climbed the stage with the help of someone I would assume was her father.

When Michelle tried to send the girl back, Heidi yelled, "Stop!"

Michelle froze, but her lips twitched in the way they'd done whenever I'd asked her to do something. She lived to obey Forrest only. That hadn't changed.

Heidi said one more insistent thing, based on her expression to Forrest, then beckoned the girl to come closer.

Forrest addressed the crowd while Heidi spoke quietly to the little girl. "The gift has chosen another. We need your help again, true believers. Please chant with us."

Without any further prompting, the eclectic group followed Forrest's clapping hands. "Healer! Healer! Healer!"

Heidi knelt before the little girl and placed her hands on either cheek. She brought her head down until their foreheads touched. From this distance, I swore I saw a ripple pass between them. Even from the outskirts of the crowd, the pink returning to the child's pale cheeks was obvious. The girl's shoulders straightened, as Heidi's hands slipped from her cheeks. The once-sick child jumped into the air.

"Daddy!" she yelled and sprinted to the man who had held her up for Heidi to notice.

Heidi, on the other hand, collapsed. Forrest caught her before her head slammed into the pallet stage. He picked her up almost tenderly. Of course, he had to protect his talent.

His voice rose through the quieted crowd. "That is all she

can handle today. We will return tomorrow after our healer has recovered."

From the stage, a large man in khakis shouted at Forrest's retreating back. "Hey! You were supposed to heal my wife. Come back!"

Michelle slid in front of the man and pushed him to the side. She guided him around to the back of the RV with his ill wife barely keeping pace. He'd probably paid in advance, as the old woman likely had. Forrest's game hadn't changed. He simply found a new empath with an ability much more advanced than my own to work his con.

I couldn't let her go down my path. I had to find a way to show her his true self.

"Are you okay?" Amelia's voice shook me from my building anger.

"I will be."

Austin panted next to us. "Wow, that was intense. If he's your brother, can we go talk to him privately? You owe Mateo."

He wasn't wrong about that. "I do owe Mateo. What I owe him is the truth and the truth is my brother is a con artist. All of this might look real, but I travelled with him for years. He used me just like he's using Heidi. Forrest only ever thinks of one person, that's Forrest."

Austin shook his head and wouldn't meet my eye.

After guiding us safely back to the GRB, Amelia watched Austin and I looking at each other without making eye contact. "Okay, look. Austin, I've met Forrest and I can back up Fauna's story of his narcissism. But, Fauna, something definitely happened back there. I feel ridiculous saying it, but something supernatural for sure."

She wasn't wrong either. "Austin, give me a couple days to get my brother alone and figure out what he's up to. If Heidi is a legit healer, then you'll be the first one I call. I'll even help you convince Flores. Just promise me that you won't go see him alone."

His eyes narrowed, but he held out his hand. "Shake on it."

And I did. Due to the long day of shaking hands and the overwhelming atmosphere I'd just left, I couldn't tell if Austin intended on keeping to his bargain. I guessed I'd just have to trust him. This was definitely a turning point for me. I had changed. Now I had to determine if my brother had.

Chapter Nine

The next morning, I sent Amelia to the convention on her own, not wanting to accidentally run into my brother yet. I wanted to do some research first, and last night I had collapsed on my couch and not woken up until morning. Plus, I'd promised Jeff I'd open Chipped since he had an ultrasound with his wife. I still couldn't believe they were expecting their third child. With as much as they fought and as often as Jeff spent the night in the back room of the store, I couldn't figure out how this child was even conceived.

Not that I had any right to criticize someone else's relationship. Somehow, Jeff and Linda made it work while I struggled to keep dates with Tucker. We'd done little more than text each other in the last couple weeks. He'd been super busy with work, and I'd been focused on learning my new barrier techniques. Though that might all just be an excuse on my end. That man made all of me tingle in the best sort of way. But as soon as other emotions started kicking in, the intensity overwhelmed my carefully constructed protections.

Seeing my brother yesterday could explain some of these tendencies. When you were betrayed so young by your closest family members, it made it rather difficult to trust again. I'd come such a long way recently though. After telling my best friends about my empathic abilities and having them immediately accept me, I'd started to believe maybe I could be me and have people stay. Maybe I wasn't giving Tucker enough credit. I could, after all, sense his sincerity, but mixed in was distraction and doubt. I didn't know if it was my close relation to him or the fact that what I wanted fought with what I feared, but I couldn't read him as clearly as I could a complete stranger.

As the displays flickered to life and the register sang its "I'm awake" song, my phone rotated in my hand as if it could make up my mind for me. This was ridiculous. I could just text him.

Me: *Hey, are you busy tonight?*

When I didn't see blinking dots right away, I tucked the device in my back pocket and busied myself with dusting the shelves.

My heart just about skipped a beat when my phone dinged. Fumbled from my pocket, the screen flashed a notification from Jeff. Clicking the button brought up Jeff and Linda with a black-and-white ultrasound picture between them. *It's a girl*, the caption read. I couldn't imagine ever having children. If nothing else, I couldn't risk passing on my empathy. Yet, something about the couple excited about creating new life enticed me.

That was when I noticed how the pic definitely showed the baby had female anatomy.

I texted back: *Please tell me you're hiding that and not embarrassing the poor child before she's born.*

Realizing I was a bit of a moron sometimes, I replied quickly: *Congratulations on the new addition!*

Jeff's answer didn't seem bothered by my rudeness: *Cindy is so excited. Now she won't be the only female presence in the house.*

I laughed: *With two older brothers to contend with, that little girl will probably be tougher than all of you combined.*

Jeff lol'd: *I'll be into work after lunch.*

With still no response from Tucker, I didn't have anywhere else to go: *Take your time. I've got it covered over here.*

Luckily, before I could stress more and start scrubbing the bathroom, a customer rang the bell. I welcomed the distraction and dived into their laptop lock out. As if the first customer opened the floodgates, the door chimed at a pretty steady rate until after lunch. It was a great Tuesday. Imagine what business could be like if I earned contracts from a company or two.

The bell jingled as Jeff came in, cuing a rumbling in my stomach that I'd missed lunch. A glance at the clock told me it was just past 1 p.m. I could probably head downtown and grab a bite to eat and see about getting a few of those companies to sign on the dotted line. I could step behind the GRB and see if Forrest was busy, I mean if I had to. If I didn't, Austin would. I couldn't let him get caught up in Forrest's aura.

Jeff beamed with pure joy, enough to tickle my toes. I couldn't recall the last time I'd sensed such a strong emotion of any type from him. "You really wanted the baby to be a girl, didn't you?"

"What?" He rubbed the sympathy fifteen pounds he'd gained over the past couple months. I thought that was a myth—showed what I knew. "Oh, the baby. Linda is thrilled. I'm just happy she looks healthy. This pregnancy has been harder on her, and I couldn't bear to lose her."

His pure joy at the health of his partner I thought he barely tolerated made me rub my back pocket where my phone sat, quiet. *Wow. Another first for me.* I envied Jeff.

"Anything exciting happen today?" He laughed before he got the whole sentence out.

I rolled my eyes. I'd definitely need to do the face time with my potential new clients. Jeff was a talented and efficient tech when it came to fixing technology, but his bedside manner needed some work. "Actually it's been busy. The active tickets are in the system."

My phone rang, and I almost jumped out of my skin. It couldn't be Tucker. He would have texted first. I nodded toward a customer who tried to get our attention by the revamped laptops for sale. Jeff took the hint, and he was in such a good mood, he didn't even argue.

The phone screen told me Flores was calling. I answered it as I moved toward the backroom, just in case I needed privacy. "What's up, Flores? Did you reschedule the prison visit?" I wondered if I should warn him about Austin and his belief in my brother's con.

His voice somehow calmed me even though it was all business. "No, but we do have a case we'd like a second opinion on?"

"We?"

He cleared his throat, and I heard the distinct flip to speaker phone.

Then a voice I didn't expect to talk respectfully to me came over the line. "Uh, Fauna, I don't know how you do what you do, but you have natural instincts or you're just a muse for Flores or whatever and I don't like it." Detective Collins paused as if to make sure I understood he was still in charge and the world made complete sense. I could probably demonstrate what I could do all day but Flores's matter-of-fact partner would find a reason to explain it away that made sense within his limited world view.

Was that what I was doing with Forrest? Heidi was doing something real on that stage, even if I couldn't nail down exactly what it was.

Detective Collins continued, "But I accept that it's effective, and I'm desperate."

Though he growled the words and I couldn't sense his emotions over the phone, I knew Collins well enough to realize how difficult it was for him to ask for help. That didn't mean I wasn't going to give him a hard time. "Huh, you need me? Fine. Let me check my calendar. And my going rate is applicable."

"Going rate?" Panic seeped into Collins's voice along with a healthy dose of *fuck this shit*. "No way am I—"

Flores somehow managed to hide the amusement he surely

felt from his next statement. "She takes payment in coffee and the occasional pastry."

He ruined Collins's torment way too early. I wanted it to last a bit longer. "Seriously though, I'm busy this afternoon. Amelia is expecting me back at the GRB for the tech convention."

A horn honked from just outside my store. Annoyance creased my forehead as I moved to the front. That kind of behavior wasn't going to get good service for any customer. A handsome, young, dark-skinned man pushed his overweight, pasty, middle-aged companion from the horn of his Ford Fusion. The fact they came to my work to pick me up made it obvious this was a bit more urgent than the two were letting on.

"You're outside my work."

Flores saluted me from the driver's side. "We're outside your work."

Ha, I knew one more way I could make sure Collins took me seriously. "Okay, fine, I'll go, but I want shotgun."

Collins grumbled as he practically kicked his door open. "Little girl who thinks she can just demand things. Well, I think—"

I hung up the phone before even I blushed at the obscenities about to leak from his mouth.

Chapter Ten

My nerves picked at my senses relentlessly when Flores swung his car onto the private, live-oak lined driveway. I knew where we were. With my emotions out of control, I couldn't sense anything the detectives felt. I never imagined crossing this threshold again. Sweat dripped down my back even though the air conditioning was on full blast.

I seriously needed to start asking more questions before accepting an offer from Flores. Wanting to help and being forced to face your own demons were two different categories of pain. Plus, what kind of crazy coincidence was this that Forrest was in town and I was about to face the family we wronged so egregiously that I left Forrest for good? What if a servant remembered me? I spent a lot of time on the property at one point. I pulled my hair down to hide as much of my face as I could.

I didn't want to tell Flores or Collins anything about my past dealings with this family. Flores would never look at me the same way again, and I don't think I could take it. "So were you going to fill me in or let me stumble around in the dark here?"

Collins snickered from the back. "Aren't you just supposed to know things?"

You know, I really hated smart-ass skeptics. You could not believe without being a dick about it. I might have been using my empathic abilities for good—at least I was trying to—but I would gladly trade them all away for a normal life where I had no idea what other people were feeling and no object held emotional time bombs waiting for me to touch them. I didn't choose this bullshit. "Look. I'm not going to be of any use to you if I'm so angry that I can't separate my own emotions from whatever it is you want me to read."

The anger did help break up the overbearing guilt, however. But I wasn't about to let Collins know he helped. At least I never met any other family members. She said they wouldn't approve. They were right not to approve.

Flores stopped the car before an inner gate I didn't remember last time I was here. "This was my idea, Fauna. Collins caught this case years ago, and we've discovered a new lead."

Case? What was happening here? Suicides didn't qualify as cases, did they?

Collins leaned forward and waved a hand around the property that must have been worth a fortune this close to downtown. "Though they're stupid rich, some awful stuff has happened to this family."

I couldn't pretend to know nothing. What would happen if I slipped and said something? These two detectives weren't stupid, and Flores had already looked at me a second too long when my foot tapped aggressively as we turned toward this street. Yet I couldn't confess I knew the matriarch, Sylvia Remington, because I'd been the one who lied to her while trying to be kind. My attempt ended in her death. I might not have pulled the trigger but her death was my fault nonetheless. It was the entire reason I left Forrest and the con life he'd set up for me. I used the money I'd earned through other people's pain to pay for college and to open Chipped.

A good chunk of that came from poor Sylvia. Whatever her

family suffered from now, I owed it to her to help them find true peace, not the bullshit I pulled on that kind woman.

Now I just had to pray none of the servants recognized me as that kid from all those years ago. I had to invoke my mom's singing voice to calm my nerves enough to ask the right questions. "I feel like I recognize this place." That was subtle enough, right?

Flores moved the car forward as the gate opened on its own, apparently satisfied with the appropriateness of the guest. "It's been featured on *Lifestyles of the Rich and the Famous* as well as multiple spots on local Houston TV. The Remington Estate has seen enough to plot several movies."

Thank God he said the name first. I didn't have to worry about faking ignorance now. "Oh, the Remingtons, now I understand the tragedy."

The trees seemed to part for dramatic effect. The glorious Victorian-style mansion bespoke of grandeur of a bygone era. The rounded tower surrounded by high-peaked gables and a grand two-story porch screamed excess. And I loved it. If I ever won the lottery, this was the type of home I wanted to build. The elaborate dentils hung from the roof lined with fish scale shingles. The deep brown of the trim color contrasted with the soft butter yellow of the siding. It was the perfect dollhouse I always wanted when I was growing up.

Collins slumped against the backseat. "It was my first murder case with my experienced partner, Grimley. He was totally convinced Sylvia Remington had taken her own life because she couldn't stand the loss of her daughter who had gone missing months earlier." He rubbed his eyes as if trying to wipe away a memory. "Then Giselle, who had been kidnapped and managed to escape, turned up two days later, alive and well. And I had to tell her what happened to her mother. Rich or not, no one should have to go through so much."

I coughed to clear the sob stuck in my throat. When I'd read of the safe return of Giselle after I'd told her mother she was dead, I almost followed Sylvia. It was my fault. If I hadn't told Sylvia her daughter would never return, she wouldn't have killed herself and Giselle would have been reunited with her only family. I was trying to end Sylvia's torment so she could move on. As long as Forrest and I had been conning people, a missing person had never returned. Forrest wanted me to string her along with false hope and promises so Sylvia would keep paying us, but I couldn't do it, not this time. I wanted to save her from pain, but instead I made it unbearable. And Sylvia decided to end it. Shit, I was not going to be able to get through this without a drink. I needed to carry around a flask for emergencies instead of relying on Amelia.

Collins continued, "But something didn't sit right with me. She had a cabinet full of guns, but she'd slit her wrists."

My forehead tightened as I digested what he said. The papers had said suicide but didn't specify how. I remembered distinctly holding Sylvia's hand as she leaned against my shoulder for the tech to take a tiny blood sample from her finger for DNA testing, just in case they found anything of her daughter to identify. Her fear of something piercing her skin was so intense, the memory made my stomach cramp now. She didn't have pierced ears or tattoos or anything. I could not see that woman purposefully slicing through her wrist. Collins might be on to something.

"And we never found a knife or razor or anything else around the body, but whatever did it had a serrated edge, the coroner was sure of it." Collins had a hand on the door latch as Flores stopped in front of the stepped entryway shaded by the massive porch. "Grimley said a servant or someone must have cleaned up after her, which we'd seen before in wealthier households. The family reputation must outlast the individual or some such nonsense."

Now listening more intently, I had to know why the change all of a sudden. "If this happened years ago and it was ruled a suicide, why are we here now?"

Flores took over. "You know the case I caught Sunday that

cut our trip short? The MO was exactly the same: slit wrists, no serrated weapon nearby that could have caused the injury, and a very peaceful scene. Not explainable as a suicide, but not chaotic enough to point to homicide."

"Just too many questions," Collins said as he opened my door. "Which apparently is where you come in. Flores seems to think you might be able to figure something out that all of my training and experience couldn't."

Jealous much? Look if you want this damn ability, I'll gladly hand it over and move on with my life. At least, that was what I wanted to shout. Instead I said, "I'll do what I can."

The first time I'd climbed these steps, Forrest and I had never seen such glamour. We'd been traveling around the south conning one group after another but had never found such an affluent target. It terrified me to be caught, especially with a case so high profile. Sylvia's daughter had been missing for two months when we were called in. Apparently, our reputation for finding the truth had preceded our move to Houston. Sylvia had searched us out to help her find her daughter. She had to know what happened. The woman was relentless. I'd never seen such motherly devotion. But I knew the statistics. After two months, there was no way her daughter was alive. But Forrest had me use whatever gifts I had available to give this poor woman comfort as she went through this tough time.

Invariably, if you gave the client good news, they wrote a bigger check. So, that was what I did. I said her daughter was safe, that she was somewhere near flowing water. Meanwhile, I felt items around the house to learn more about the girl. Turned out she had a secret boyfriend I was able to tell Sylvia about, though I didn't tell her I found an impression of her daughter's first sexual encounter with this man on her mother's bed. Some things you had to keep to yourself.

The more I got to know Sylvia in person and her daughter through the memories left behind, I started to resent the younger Remington. How could she treat her mother with such distain when all this woman did was love her and try to give her every opportunity? I never found any clues to tell me what happened to Giselle, and the police found nothing when they investigated the boyfriend. But I knew the statistics, and I couldn't stand Sylvia's pain any longer.

I told her I had a vision, and her daughter was gone, moved on to the other side. I even acted as a "medium," which I'd gotten pretty good at faking over the years. Based on Sylvia's reactions to my shaky answers, I was able to guide the responses to what Sylvia felt was the truth of her daughter. She'd been one hundred percent convinced and dismissed us. Forrest was so mad, he almost called UofH and got me expelled by telling them about my lack of a high school diploma.

I promised Forrest I'd find another wealthy donor. I knew Sylvia had friends she'd recommend us to, once she was done grieving. Before we moved on to the next client, Sylvia was dead. The shock of this kind woman in so much pain over the loss of her daughter that she couldn't bear to live anymore broke me.

Forrest tried to comfort me, though after what happened next, I wasn't sure if that was because he cared or because he didn't want to lose his moneymaker. When the daughter showed up, two days after her mother died. The guilt all but broke me. If I hadn't bonded with Gina and Amelia by then, I don't think I would have recovered from that blow. If I'd just given the woman hope instead of dashed her dreams, Sylvia would still be alive today.

So I broke away from my brother, told him if he did anything to threaten my college education—the thing I grasped onto as my only way out of the con life he'd set up—then I'd go straight to the cops and tell them about all the cons we'd pulled. At that point, I'd have nothing to lose. And who do you think they'd punish harder? The poor girl who was forced to do her brother's bidding or the man who basically pimped out his sister so her sweet face and innocent eyes would fool the targets?

I had to give him credit. Forrest knew when he was beat. He

left and swore he'd never come back. Luckily I had a small bank account set up on the side, because he cleared out the one we shared before he left town.

That was almost a decade ago. Now I climbed the steps right behind the actual authorities. I prayed a stranger opened the door. Though I deserved condemnation, I'd prefer to not ruin my reputation with Flores so early in our relationship. Plus, I still thought about Sylvia all the time. If I could help her family find peace, I wanted to do whatever I could.

The door swung open before Collins rang the bell. I sucked in a breath as Sylvia Remington stood on the stoop and stared right at me.

Chapter Eleven

With a heavy cough, I cleared my throat to force myself to blink and take a step back. Obviously, the woman wasn't Sylvia. I needed to get my reactions under control before the perceptive Flores asked questions I wasn't ready to answer. The woman standing behind the servant who had opened the door—also a stranger to my relief—had to be Sylvia's daughter, Giselle.

The past decade had turned the bratty teenager from the pictures over the mantle into a stunning replica of her mother, though Giselle's dusty blonde hair had more color than her mother's silver had. She wore the same style of pants suit that seemed to be ever in vogue with the wealthy class. Her jewelry was understated but no doubt fine—unlike the costume jewelry adorning my ears. With a few more years and a few more worry lines, Giselle could be her mother's twin.

The grand foyer had the same polished marble from floor to ceiling that I remembered. The flowers in the elaborate vase on the central table were the same red and white roses. Well, probably not the same because they were certainly real. That authentic rose smell couldn't be faked, not with the most expensive candle. It looked like Giselle hadn't touched a thing since she returned home. She'd kept everything exactly as her mother had had it.

Thinking of Sylvia made me hold my hands tightly against my side. I didn't know what impressions might have been left by the grieving mother since I'd betrayed her trust. I might deserve the punishment, but I certainly wouldn't welcome it.

"Ms. Remington," Collins's voice lowered an octave when he took on a professional air I wasn't aware he possessed. He did care about this case. "I'm Detective Collins. We spoke on the phone earlier."

"Yes, Detective. Giselle is fine." She raised her eyebrows at Flores and me, awaiting an introduction.

Collins didn't seem to get the hint. Luckily, Flores did, and he elbowed his older partner. "Oh, this is my partner, Detective Flores." Collins looked at me for a second. I could feel his indecision as he tried to decide what to call me.

Flores stepped in before he flubbed anything. "It's a pleasure to meet you. I only wish it were under better circumstances. This is a consultant who specializes in difficult cases, Fauna Young."

A bit of shock came from the servant as she closed the door behind us. She must have recognized my name. Oh shit, maybe I should have come up with a pseudonym. I turned as if to run back out the door and saw the servant shaking her thumb and cursing the lock under her breath. I had to bite my tongue to stifle a nervous laugh. She'd pinched her finger in the door. My name hadn't caused any reaction. If I was jumpy the whole time, this was going to be a long day.

I did, however, have to make sure that Giselle didn't find my name familiar. I reached out my hand to shake hers. I swallowed a sob as she even smelled like her mother, musky vanilla with a faint whiff of baby powder under it all. To her credit, she didn't hesitate and grasped my fingers in a firm grip. A pain stabbed me from the back of the eyes and a light tensing of my jaw told me Giselle was sad, but I didn't sense any anger or resentment.

There was a bit of tingling in my fingers mixed with a bit of tightening of my gut. I was pretty sure it was not because she recognized me but because she was curious about why the detectives had requested a visit. Her next comment verified my guess.

"Now that we're all acquainted, may I ask why you're here?" Giselle managed to keep her face completely still though my throbbing eyes told me sadness wracked her.

Detective Collins took the lead. "Ms. Remington, we'd like to review your mother's case. Your formal complaint on our ruling of suicide has stayed on the record." He obviously couldn't call her by her given name. "Full disclosure, I was here as a rookie detective and something didn't sit right with me either."

My throat swelled slightly as Giselle must have satisfied her curiosity. What I sensed must have been her recognizing Collins, but not being able to place him. "I remember you," she said as she lead us into the parlor Forrest and I had spent so much time in. "You didn't say much all those years ago."

Collins's gaze fell to the ornate Oriental rug that probably cost more than my car. "I was new."

I'd never seen him so humble. There was more to the grumpy, old detective than I'd chosen to see.

"I'm not sure what I can help you with." Giselle motioned toward a sofa that would have looked natural in a French palace. I probably could have traced the intricate garden pattern in my sleep. When she took the same chair with dark, stained mahogany legs that her mother always chose, I had to stifle a tear. I brushed my hand on the arm as I walked by. I couldn't stop myself. As I suspected, it was a remnant, though a subtle one I'd not have noticed if I hadn't physically touched it. The image of Forrest, thin and pale, with me sitting beside him, hair down to my waist, flashed to my conscious. I ripped my hand away before my locked jaw blossomed to close my throat. Sylvia's sadness never left my memory. I didn't need the visceral reminder now. Apparently, her daughter took more than looks from her mother.

As Collins took a seat, Flores held a hand out for me to wait. "Would it be possible for Fauna and I to visit the bathroom?" He didn't clarify which one.

By the look on Giselle's face, he didn't need to. She swallowed deeply and nodded to the same servant who had opened the door. "Please show the detective upstairs."

"Right this way, Detective," the servant said, her eyes downcast and cheeks flushed.

Flores waved me forward. A step behind the servant in black pants and a white polo, I wished she had a name tag. It felt odd having someone show me around without knowing her name. As we left the emotional heaviness of the parlor, a bit of tightness cramped my lower abdomen. I might have been wrong about this servant. She might recognize me.

After swallowing my own embarrassment that I didn't recognize her at all, I realized I had to be wrong. She was too young to have been there ten years ago. She was definitely younger than me and the only female servant I remembered had been at least twenty years older. It was probably my guilt making me feel things that weren't there. I needed to get a handle on it before it influenced anything I learned in the bathroom.

Flores pulled a file from his jacket. "Do you want to see the scene before going in?"

It showed how much he trusted my ability that he was willing to give me a peek and didn't think it would lead me to fake a vision. Considering what I did to the Remingtons, I felt like I didn't deserve such consideration. Though this was my chance to make it right, so maybe I should take whatever advantage I could get to help interpret whatever I see. Then again, my own guilt might flare and block anything else.

While I considered his offer, I crossed the threshold from the marble floors that continued down the upstairs hallway from the foyer below to the likely imported clay tile of the bathroom. The space was as big as my kitchen and living room combined.

After a deep breath, I shook my head at Flores's offer. "Let me do my thing first. Alone."

From the hallway, Flores didn't even blink as he opened his arm to encourage the servant to exit so he could close the door.

"I have it, sir," she insisted.

So Flores walked through first, and the petite woman slammed the door and locked it from the inside. Then she turned to me with a look of abstract hate that cut through all of my barriers with its pointed intensity. A searing cramp gripped my abdomen and tugged on my scarred tissue. I couldn't think of anything else but the pain.

Chapter Twelve

I crumbled in half and hit the floor as all of my organs squeezed at once. Flores banged on the door and shouted. A few words managed to leave through my gritted teeth. "What? What do you want?"

My wheezing voice didn't seem to put a dent in her anger, neither did my seemingly inexplicable illness that caused me to curl up on the fine Italian marble. My shoulders burned from the servant's sheer loathing. It wasn't often I experienced pure, raw emotion. Most people kept it pretty much under control. This woman had lost it. And all of my old injuries flared with the intensity.

"How dare you come back here? How dare you return to the scene of the crime?"

"I don't ..." Well, shit, my stomach cramped so severely I was scared I'd soil my pants.

"My mother worked the estate when you and your brother—if he even was your brother—came here when Ms. Giselle had gone missing. My mother told me everything. Forrest and Fauna Young, she said, two con artists who convinced the mistress to give them all sorts of money for fake comfort until she couldn't take the pain anymore and ended it all." She stomped her foot, and I flinched as if she'd kicked me.

So far, she only spoke the truth, which made me almost wish she *had* kicked me. Heaven knows, I deserved it.

My mother's voice strengthened without me even calling it to the forefront. Habits really were forming into instincts just as the Collected told me they would. I used the distraction to separate my own feelings of guilt from the servant's seething anger. My guts loosened up enough for me to uncurl and sit. "I'm so sorry for what happened. I was trying to comfort her. Bring her peace."

"No, you weren't!" she yelled. "I won't let you con the daughter like you did the mother."

"I'm so sorry about what happened. I would never do anything like that again." The words sounded lame and useless, but I didn't know what else to say. "The cops are reopening the case to see what really happened."

The young servant stood high. "Is that why you're here? To throw them off your scent, because you actually killed the mistress? My mother knew you had something more than just words; she always said she saw a young woman sneaking off the property that night before she found Mrs. Remington in there." She nodded to the bathtub behind us.

Tears dripped down her cheeks taking some of her anger with it. It takes a lot of energy to maintain that level of emotion. She must have run out. Maybe I could get through to her now. Barriers popped into my mind. The whole build-a-wall-in-your-brain thing worked. I just had to stay focused and not do too much decorating. Inside the cubicle of concrete, I placed my thoughts and feelings and left the maid's outside. I could do this. A bit more practice and it would be second nature.

As my body loosened from the intense cramping, I noticed the door vibrating. The banging intensified to the point I thought the wood would crack if the hinges didn't give. "Hold on, Flores. Everything is fine. I've got it."

As I rose to my feet, the door quieted.

"You have five minutes, then I'm coming in." Flores's protective nature was just as comforting as Amelia's. But this time, I knew I could take care of myself. I just had to get it together.

I took both of the servant's hands in mine. My guts still twisted, but I'd managed to put up enough barriers while she talked to make it more diagnostic instead of debilitating. Underneath the anger was loss. She was certainly mad about what she perceived my crime to be, but there was something else, something fueling the overreaction. I took an educated guess. "What happened to your mother?"

It was her turn to collapse to the floor. I crouched beside her, never losing contact.

"She never forgave herself. She'd gone outside to have a smoke while the mistress bathed. It was part of her routine, but she said the mistress was acting very strange that day." She blinked and looked out of the window, refusing to look me in the eyes.

For not the first time, I wished my empathy could take away her pain instead of just share it. "It's not her fault. None of it is her fault."

She continued like I hadn't said anything, "My mother never had another cigarette, but she took up drinking. Her heart failed her two years ago." Now she looked at me and ripped her hands from mine. "And it's all your fault."

She lunged at me, but it was half-hearted. I was able to dodge out of the way. She fell to the ground and smacked her head on the marble. I unlocked the door and Flores rushed in like he'd been perched on his toes waiting for the chance. Collins and Giselle stood just behind him. Giselle bit her nails while Collins's face seemed to get redder by the second.

Flores pulled the servant up off the floor and practically drug her into the hallway.

Giselle asked, "What's going on?"

The girl fought him and pointed an accusing finger at me.

"That woman conned your mother, and she's returned to con you too."

As all faces turned to me, my cheeks probably shone brighter than Collins's as I felt them burn in embarrassment. The worst was the look of sadness from Flores. I should have told him. He deserved better than to be blindsided at the scene of the crime.

Something seemed to click in Giselle's mind. "You're Forrest Young's sister?"

My jaw seemed to lock up, so I just nodded. I didn't have the energy to lie.

She kept going. "He called after I got home, after I missed seeing my mother one last time. He said he and his sister were sorry."

Forrest called? He showed sympathy? Surely that was not something a murderer would do, right?

Giselle tilted her head as if she tried to reach into my brain and understand, kind of like I did to her mother. "I always wondered what he meant. What did you do to her?"

I lied to her and told her you were never coming home. Instead of letting go and healing, she ended her life to join you. Of course, I couldn't say that. "My brother and I comforted your mother when she was hurting with your loss. Obviously, we failed."

Before they could kick me out of the house, I moved toward the bathtub. There was no way I'd let this entire day be wasted. If Forrest apologized, there was no way he was the killer. Time to fall into Sylvia's last memory, so I could add her torment to my own. It was only fair.

The servant screamed from the hallway. "And you took her money for your comfort. She must have found out about your scam and confronted you."

"No, we weren't scamming her." I found myself talking to Flores rather than the actual victims. I only cared about what he thought. "She did pay us though. She said I uniquely understood her, which I did." I stumbled over my words. I couldn't be completely obvious; it sounded ludicrous. "So she wanted to pay us like companions who helped her through a tough time."

I didn't even try to give it back though, even after I knew what I'd done. I couldn't tell her that either. "When I heard you were found, we were thrilled for her. And then we heard what happened. She must have given up." Probably because I told her you were gone. Oh God, why had I returned? I should have dove out of the moving car as soon as I realized where we were headed.

"But that's just the thing." Giselle perked up, like we were close to some sort of answer. "I called her before I even called 911. Her voice was all I wanted to hear." She flicked a tear from the corner of her eye, and her gaze focused on the bathtub. "She sounded so excited on the phone. Her relief was palpable, at least I thought it was. When I was in captivity, all I thought about was seeing her face again, to apologize for being such a spoiled brat. Why would she kill herself before we actually got back together?"

Sylvia knew her daughter was alive and she *still* killed herself? "That doesn't make any sense. Why would she end her life if she knew you were okay?" So it wasn't my fault. She didn't kill herself because I lied to her.

Hope is a strange beast. If this wasn't my fault, I could let go of a lot of guilt. Well, I could try anyway. It was time. I needed to touch that bathtub. I couldn't sense even a vibration from where I stood. I had to get closer. I lifted my eyebrows at Flores and nodded toward my target.

Before Flores found a way to get me alone in the bathroom, Giselle gave us the perfect opening. "I can't be in here anymore."

Collins crossed his arms and narrowed his eyes like he knew all along I was up to no good.

Flores's calm voice cut through Collins's anger. "You should go after her. See if she's willing to talk about that call with her mom. It's not in the file."

After giving me one more squinty stare, Collins motioned for the servant to go ahead of him. "You should go that way. No more attacking today."

Since she was outside the room, her sheer ferocity didn't overwhelm me anymore, but my shoulders still burned causing me to rub them to make it stop. With everyone else gone, I should have been able to concentrate enough to read what truly happened to Sylvia, if she left anything behind.

Flores closed the door and leaned against it. "Do you need me to go too?" His reluctance at the thought of leaving me again was obvious. Besides, I could use a bit of his calming influence.

"No." I rolled my shoulders to release some of the external tension, which only served to aggravate the torn tissue. I'd survived a serial killer; I could survive the last memory of an old friend. He looked down at the tile and crossed his ankles, looking and feeling calm. The Collected could probably learn a few relaxing techniques from him.

No more procrastination. Giselle could kick us out at any moment. I doubted I'd be invited back. I had to gather what I could now. Hovering my hands over the edge of the tub, nothing jumped out as an impression. I couldn't imagine anyone ending their life and not leaving something behind. I'd experienced remnants from much less potent emotions than that.

A pull from the base of the tub drew me to the rounded end. As I stepped over the iron claw, the pull grew more insistent. She must have been facing this way which was why I didn't sense anything from the center of the room.

Before second guessing myself, I touched the cold surface.

My body vibrated with heat. At first I thought it was warm water enveloping my body until I realized half of me was out of the water. Everything that was happening to my body felt so good, I didn't want to separate this time. But I was a professional now and forced myself to pull back like I was watching someone else's dream.

Judging by the hair style of the man between her legs, this memory was formed decades before Sylvia's death. And what they were doing together was so much more than satisfying lust. They were deeply in love. The sensation thrilled every fiber in my body more deeply than any sex I'd ever had, and the handsome man was barely touching her with his talented tongue. When the dark-haired stud looked up, bubbles cradled his head like some sort of sexual angel.

"Forever then?" the woman asked, displaying a ring with a huge diamond that looked familiar to me.

"And then some," he said in a deep, lustful tone.

His handsome face sparked my memory. Sylvia always put a hand on a framed picture beside her armchair. Though the man in that photo had wrinkles around the eyes and a bald pate, he had the same chiseled chin and high cheekbones of the young man in the tub.

Suddenly feeling like an intruder in Sylvia's life, I tore my hand from the cast iron. My flushed cheeks burned as I shook my hands to stave off the lust still raging in my body.

Flores didn't move from his casual pose against the door. "What did you see?"

It was so nice to have someone who believed me, but right now, I wasn't up for sharing the details. "Nothing from Sylvia's final night." My fingers twitched to touch the tub again. I really did need to call Tucker.

"Is that normal for ..." he trailed off, but I knew he wanted to know if nothing left behind was normal for a suicide.

"I wish I could give you a definitive answer, but, thank god, I haven't encountered enough of a sample size to make a hypothesis."

"Fair enough." He sounded so understanding, but I felt his disappointment. My nerves were raw and open. I could sense the angry servant talking with Collins down the hallway. Dammit, if this gift couldn't give answers, then what good was it. This helplessness made me feel like a child and I slammed my teeth together just like I used to. Pain shot through my bottom lip as I caught it in my temper tantrum.

"Dammit," I said out loud this time. I pulled a Kleenex from the dispenser put-together people seemed to always have on the back of their toilet and leaned toward the mirror. As I dipped at the blood, I felt that same familiar sensation I had on the street a few days ago and at the rally with my brother.

Had he been in this bathroom? I knew I hadn't seen it before, but it wasn't like we never went anywhere without each other. But this was Sylvia's private chambers. She had countless privies for us to do our business in. Maybe Forrest came in here to steal valuables? That I wouldn't put past my brother.

The full impact of sensing Forrest at both places where unexplained suicides occurred was too uncomfortable to think about. It was true Sylvia might have reported us to someone of authority, but what threat would the homeless volunteer have offered. Plus, my brother had shaky morals when it came to other people's money, but he never hurt anyone physically.

Well, except for our dad that one time.

None of which I was ready to confess to Flores about. I'd already laid enough on him for one day.

With one hand on the doorknob, he searched my eyes. "Are you sure there's nothing?"

How could I tell him Forrest might be involved? Though there was something odd going on and I at least had to question him about it. Even with everything he'd put me through and done to me, I couldn't just turn him over to the police. I trusted Flores, but Forrest was blood.

But I couldn't lie to Flores either. "Nothing from Sylvia beyond a very pleasant memory involving her husband."

At Flores's lifted eyebrow, my cheeks burned again. Austin was a lucky man. Flores's tanned skin and smoldering eyes lined him up as the stereotypical strong and silent type. Which reminded me of Austin's obsession with Forrest and his new side show. I had to find out what was going on and how Forrest was involved, not only to find the truth for Sylvia's daughter, but to prevent Austin from making a huge mistake.

Chapter Thirteen

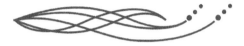

After the most awkward drive back to the store to get my car that I'd ever experienced, I immediately set out for the GRB. I had to confront my brother. The nagging feeling of his possible guilt ate at my conscience as much, if not more so, than Flores's accusing silence. Collins absolutely fumed. I'd hoped to win him over, but I only pushed him farther away.

Flores might believe in my ability, but that didn't mean he'd use me if he couldn't trust me. But could I hand my brother over as a suspect? Especially when I didn't truly know his involvement beyond a vague suspicion that felt completely ridiculous because my brother couldn't kill anyone. Could he?

The parking lot behind the GRB still held the trailer I'd seen Forrest and Heidi enter, but no one answered the door. Oddly, I didn't sense any sort of presence left behind. Maybe whatever left it had to be tied to an emotion like with normal impressions. Well, that was new. I considered something about my life experience as normal.

Back in my vehicle, I circled the area to see if a crowd gathered somewhere else, eager to be conned by Forrest's pretty words. East Downtown, or EaDo as the cool kids called it, had really grown since the last time I'd spent time down here. Lots of little bars and brew pubs and eclectic restaurants dotted around the old Chinese shops. The girls and I would have to explore one night.

Before I decided to stop and have a drink, St. Benedict's sign flashed from the next block, garnering my attention. My car seemed to make its own decision as it turned down the one-way heading for the street parking around the back of the repurposed church.

If I couldn't find Forrest, I could at least walk by the place I sensed the familiar presence to verify it was the same as at Sylvia's. Mind you, it didn't mean my brother was a killer, but if the two sensations didn't match at all, I could at least know I was experiencing something new and it had nothing to do with him.

After awkwardly parallel parking—I'd probably never get comfortable with it no matter how long I lived in the city—and paying the solar-powered machine for the privilege, I made my way around the corner. In front of the weathered granite steps leading to the grand entrance, a group of people milled about in the shade, though not nearly as many as I'd seen in the past.

"Fauna?"

Of all the things I thought I'd experienced, I didn't think anyone would know me here. I turned around to see Gina pulling a cardboard box from her back seat. "Gina? What are you doing here?"

"I volunteer here remember?" She handed me the box—that was much lighter than I expected—then reached in to grab another. "The better question is what are you doing here?"

I couldn't very well say, *I came to see if my brother could possibly be a murderer.* Why did it feel like I was always keeping secrets? My life truly wasn't that interesting. At least, it didn't used to be. So instead, I said, "Searching for my brother."

"Oh, I thought maybe you were here to see Tucker."

My mind temporarily froze. "Why would Tucker ...?" I didn't even know how to finish that sentence. Tucker'd never mentioned volunteering at the homeless shelter. Though in his defense, when we were together, we didn't do a ton of talking.

Seemingly unbothered by my stammering, Gina said, "He's been in and out of the shelter for a week trying to figure out what's making the homeless sick." As we made our way to the door, Gina cocked her head at me. "Did you say brother? Forrest or Hawke?"

Gina was really the best of us. "I forgot you still call him Hawke."

"Well, that's his name, isn't it?"

"Sure, it's his name, but it never fit. He doesn't have any predator instincts, which is why we call him Sparrow."

"He hates that you know."

I did know but for some reason never stopped. We hadn't spoken since last Christmas. We weren't estranged; we just weren't vital to each other's every day. Separating from each other was probably how we survived mostly sane. It was either that or talk about our family dynamic authentically. Oh man, I had a lot to talk about with the Collected on Friday.

The lady at the front desk waved at Gina, who said with a nod in my direction, "Good afternoon, Priya. She's with me."

Priya, whose wrinkled eyes and hands said fifties while her deep brown hair without a hint of gray said thirties, smiled at us. But it was weak, and her reddened eyes and swollen cheeks spoke of recent crying. "Of course, anything for you, Gina. But if she's going to be a regular, she'll have to go through the background check."

Setting the box on the counter, Gina hugged Priya. "It's just so awful."

Fresh tears popped from Priya's eyes. "I thought I was done crying. I don't know what we're going to do without him."

The back of my eyes throbbed with deep sadness. For an empath, sometimes I was an insensitive jerk. I'd forgotten the murder victim from two days ago was a beloved volunteer at St.

Benedict's. "I'm so sorry for your loss." Such an inadequate thing to say, but what else was there.

When Gina picked back up her box, I followed her into a hallway that looked more mundane than I expected for either a church or a homeless shelter.

"Have they learned anything new about his death?"

Gina paused with her back to a door that swung slightly. "Nothing that I've heard. I thought you would hear something before we did."

I simply shook my head. I had no idea what I knew or didn't at this point.

Gina's brow, as modest as it was, furrowed. "Wait. Did you say Forrest is back in town? Didn't he promise to never come back to Houston?"

"He did." And don't think I wasn't sore about that. But I had so much more to worry about, like if he was a murderer. A sneaky one at that. "Nevertheless, he's here. Michelle is still with him, but his new girl can 'heal.'" I air-quoted with my fingers, which was much less effective since they were occupied with a cardboard box. "What's in this anyway?"

"Oh," Gina leaned back swinging the door open for me to go through. "My class decorated paper bags for the children at the shelter to carry their lunch in."

I'd been so busy worried about my problems, I'd forgotten St. Benedict's mission. As I entered the commercial kitchen, I took note of the people standing on the other side of the counter with cafeteria style trays. Though men were still the majority, this line also held a substantial grouping of women and children. It was just like I remembered.

I nudged Gina's hip with mine. "You are some sort of super-hero, my friend. I never help anyone."

She smiled with her raised eyebrow that always told me I was missing something. My college GPA would engulf hers, yet she was the one who always seemed to know something I didn't.

"Seriously?" she said as she motioned for me to set my box

next to hers in a pantry full of paper goods. "You caught a serial killer last year."

I scoffed. "Yes, I very cleverly let him use my body as a pin cushion until Flores found us and stopped him."

Tears popped into Gina's eyes. "I'm so sorry to bring it up, but you know damn well you did more than that."

A throbbing kicked up behind my eyes again. I'm such an asshole sometimes. I made Gina swear, out loud, in public. "Oh, Gina, please don't be upset. I was trying to make light of my own accomplishments. I mean, I did throw him off of me by making him feel the pain he inflicted on me. That's something, right?"

She squeezed my shoulders, careful not to hit bare skin below my sleeves. "Right. Now help me make sandwiches."

I could always hit that spot outside on my way out. "It would be my pleasure." Plus, maybe I could get a tour and see if I could sense that familiar presence inside.

Gina piped up. "Want a tour first? A lot has changed since our college years."

And they said I was the mind reader. "I would love one."

She cocked her head at me and crossed her arms. "Do you need to do something to like prepare? You never know what the people we help here are going through at any given moment."

That was when I realized I hadn't been inundated when I crossed the threshold. Between my familial distraction and the overload I experienced at the Remingtons, my sensitivity was at a low murmur. "I think I'm good." I tried to ensure my voice flowed with confidence.

Gina cocked her head but chose to believe me. She always did. "Okay, but before we go, there's been a bit of a condition running through the homeless population. That's what Tucker's looking into. We're not sure if it's a flu or what's causing it, but we've taken extra precautions." She handed me a blue and white mask and indicated a box of disposable gloves.

"Thank you?" I didn't have time to get sick. Maybe I'd take a raincheck.

A woman with short brown hair and facial features I couldn't identify under the mask leaned her head into the pantry. "Oh, Gina, Priya said you'd come in today. That same computer won't connect to the internet. We don't know what we're doing wrong, and there's a line trying to finish applying for disability."

I couldn't believe what I was hearing. "Wait. You're the computer expert around here?"

I felt Gina smile though I couldn't see her perfect teeth. "Well, hanging with you and Amelia had to have some benefit. I'm at least not afraid of the things anymore. Turn it off and on, press buttons, and search Google. It's really not that hard."

She winked at me as I tried to realign my tilted world. A tingling in my breasts made me do a double take. Who was feeling lust?

The short-haired woman stood in the doorway of the pantry with her hip cocked and one eyebrow raised. "Who's the new girl?"

Gina laughed. "This is my friend Fauna. Fauna meet Jacinta, our very own welcoming committee, whether you want to be welcomed or not."

"Oh, I feel welcomed." And I certainly did. If women were my thing, I'd have gotten her number right then. Time to change the subject. "But it seems computer issues are the big problem right now. At least, a problem I could probably solve for you. Tech and I have an understanding."

Jacinta shifted her weight to her other hip and opened an arm to the exit. "I would be honored to watch you work, Fauna, friend of Gina's."

With an eye roll and a gentle push, Gina guided us to the cafeteria where multiple round tables surrounded by metal folding chairs were set up on industrial white tile. Everything was tightly packed in, but the high ceilings of the old church made the space feel open instead of claustrophobic. One corner had been cordoned off with dividers like any cubicle farm, though these were composed of clear plastic instead of the weird cloth padding that was typical.

As we hit the swell of people, I realized my abilities weren't quite as dull as I'd hoped. Sensations rippled through my body as one emotion after another washed over me. Anger with a clench of my jaw morphed to fear and a twist of my gut. A little boy in pants two sizes too big and a shirt two sizes too small danced beside what I assumed was his mother with a banana in one hand while holding up his pants with the other. Their contentedness washed away the negativity so successfully, I wanted to sit down and join them as a barrier to the negative emotions. I resisted though because one replaced another and then another as we made our way through the crowd.

We wandered quite a bit after my dad died. Mom, Forrest, Sparrow, and I usually found somewhere to lay our heads, but nothing that would be mistaken for stability. We'd stayed at more than one shelter as Mom struggled to make ends meet. Now that I knew more about what I was, I had a feeling Mom struggled just as badly with her own empathic issues. I couldn't imagine raising a family on my own while trying to maintain some semblance of sanity. Spikes of disorganized, but intense, emotions strewn along the outskirts of the mass of people reminded me many of them suffered from mental issues as well.

The sudden urge to do something, to help them as I wished someone would have stepped up to help us, swelled in my chest. The newfound motivation brought me focus, and I almost beat Jacinta to the computer bank. The bulky monitors that took up much of the space on the modest desks along with the rectangular boxes with fans so loud it was a wonder anyone could hear anything made me feel as if I'd traveled back in time.

I whistled at the antiques before me. "Gina, if you were getting these relics to work, I'm tipping my hat to you. What are they used for anyway?" I couldn't imagine using them for anything more than paperweights since they'd take up all the room on the desk. I wouldn't resell any of these in my shop, not even under consignment.

Gina pointed to a station in use by a frazzled woman next to a teenager begging her to hurry up as she struggled with a toddler on her hip. The monitor scrolled in a way that would give me a headache within a minute and a half. "Job applications, disability paperwork, temporary housing, schoolwork sometimes. Everything's online now. Without access to a computer on the internet, no one can get any assistance."

Jacinta leaned well within my personal space. Her friendly vibes felt good though, so I didn't back off. "It's us or the public library. And the library doesn't feed them or offer a place to wash clothes."

Guilt ate at me when I realized I had been ignoring a problem I could actually help with. Just a few blocks away, IT specialists and programmers and high-level businesspeople walked around with laptops, each worth more than all of this equipment tied together. There had to be a way to get them to donate to help these people in desperate need.

Direction and a goal helped me shake out of my guilt and get to work. "Well, I've got this if you can handle the sandwiches, Gina."

"I might not be the gourmet in our group, but kids' meals are right up my alley." Gina tapped my shoulder and motioned toward another door. "Before you get started, you might want to say hi to your beau."

Chapter Fourteen

Startled by a familiar feeling of warmth that trickled through my fingertips, I looked up to see Tucker in full doctor mode, scrubs and all, walking through a side door. Even with his mask on, I knew he had a soft smile on his lips because his eyes were slightly crinkled on the edges. He always smiled like that. His quiet confidence made my heart skip a beat.

Then it dropped to the soles of my feet. Oh God, that man was way too good for me. At one late night chat session—when I really should have left but found myself stuck in his arms—he told me about how he was a disappointment to his family because he was just a doctor, an ER doctor no less, not like a famous cardiologist or running a cancer treatment center for ultimate fortune. The rest of Tucker's family were lawyers, like names on the side of a building lawyers, going back three generations. His brother and sister had dutifully followed the family legacy, but Tucker decided he wanted to help people.

A sad beep from a computer shutting itself off lifted my spirits a bit. I guessed it was time to earn my place in this world. I'd get the shelter stocked with reliable equipment and fast internet.

What was I doing? Usually, I'd run away when it got too real with a man, and now I was trying to *earn* his respect. This was ridiculous. I needed a drink.

Tucker spotted Gina first. I blamed the mask. "Hey, I didn't expect you here today. Get out of school early?"

Gina laughed, and I had to swallow an unjustified touch of jealousy. "No, it's after four."

He looked at his watch as his eyebrows reached into his sun-kissed bangs. "Damn, where did the time go?"

I couldn't stand him not seeing me any longer. I cleared my throat and stood straight up from my crouch beside the desk.

"Fauna?" His voice was laced with surprise. I was so relieved to feel my toes tingle at his happiness. He was glad to see me.

Gina waved to us as Jacinta pushed her toward the kitchen. "I'll catch y'all on the other side. Maybe we could do dinner downtown when the shelter closes."

Tucker and I both nodded but our focus didn't wane from each other. What was this I was feeling? I'd never experienced it before, between my nipples tingling and my stomach seeming to rise into my throat. Why had I procrastinated calling him? At that very moment, I couldn't recall why I'd ever left his presence at all.

At the same time, we said, "I didn't expect to see you here."

I waved our words away before the cuteness killed me. "Turns out St. Benedict's is in serious need of computer repair."

Tucker's hand drifted toward mine, though the gloves made it awkward and he didn't quite grab my fingers. "You'll whip them into shape in no time, I'm sure. I wish my visit was so easily quantified. I haven't found any answers."

Suddenly on alert, I pointed at the gloves and masks. "These will help right?"

With his hands on his hips like Superman, he surveyed the crowd in the cafeteria. "They're just a precaution. I'm not even sure they're necessary since we can't figure out what's causing the symptoms. My ER has been inundated with a kind of wasting illness. None of them are improving and they all seem to have a connection to St. Benedict's. But that's all we can figure out."

My arms wrapped around my gut as my own fear overcame any influence from the outside. "Is it safe to be here?"

Without looking at me, Tucker shrugged. "I just don't know. We couldn't narrow it down to a known pathogen so I'm here gathering samples from services and the food to see if we can find something there."

When he met my eyes, his face blanched. "Oh, Fauna, I didn't mean to frighten you. None of the staff have fallen ill which makes me think it's not in the building at all. We're just crossing off all of the variables."

My knee started to vibrate regardless of his comforting words. He pulled me in for a hug, and I melted into his arms. Huh, that's why romances used that phrase. That was exactly what it felt like as all my fears washed away, replaced by his tenderness.

He continued, "Plus, when I called a colleague in Dallas for a consultation, he said they'd had the same issue a week ago and still don't have answers."

"Excuse me, doctor." An older woman, whose mottled skin attested to her many hours spent in the sun, tugged on Tucker's sleeve. Odd that I didn't feel her approach at all. My abilities were all over the place this week: either super sensitive or completely blind.

My stomach felt empty as Tucker separated to address the woman. "Yes, ma'am. How can I help you?"

"Ma'am? Henrietta's fine, though my friends call me Scout because I'm always prepared." Her voice cracked but it didn't seem to bother her. "I heard you talk about the Wasting."

Tucker released me completely and offered Henrietta a chair at the desk of the broken computer. "Yes, Scout. We're doing everything we can to find an answer. Are you feeling okay?"

"I am fine, doctor. Better than you, I'd say."

Tucker sat in the chair next to her and leaned in. His attentiveness made me proud, as if I was somehow part of it. I rubbed my forehead to ward off the threat of tears for no reason at all. Seeing Forrest again and Sylvia's daughter and all of the reminders of my past digressions had me on edge and unstable. It was time to head home, put my feet up, and indulge in a bottle of Sauvignon Blanc.

Tucker's voice tried to calm me again, but my own emotional state resisted its power. "What did you want to tell me about the ... what did you call it?"

"The Wasting," she said again as if explaining to a child. "I know what causes it."

Tucker somehow managed to not scoff. He was a better person than I. "What causes it?"

"The Shadows."

"Shadows?" My voice might have been laced with doubt, but my memory tugged at what I'd experienced in Sylvia's bathroom.

Tucker pushed back in his chair and cracked his neck, obviously frustrated with his lack of progress in his diagnosis. But seriously, what did he expect to learn from a random old woman who flagged him down?

Henrietta responded to our disbelief by shaking her head and waving a hand. "I know it sounds crazy. And I knew you wouldn't believe me, but I had to try. The night before Xavier fell ill, Shadows walked down Main."

"Xavier." Tucker sighed more than spoke the name. "He said a sleeping angel carried by a demon visited him."

The old woman continued to shake her head. "Well, Xavier was always a little crazy. Shadows what visited him. Shadows that walk the streets most nights looking for souls. I saw 'em last night." She pulled an oval mirror with one long jagged crack from the plastic bag tied around her belt. "I flashed them with this and they ran off and left poor Xavier on the street, gasping and mumbling."

Against my better judgment, I slipped a glove off and reached for the mirror. I could see the vibrations around its metal rim. Something was on it. Maybe I could see what happened that night, get a better glimpse of the shadows. The old woman slipped it back into her pack with a squinty look at my outstretched hand.

When I backed off, she produced a single peach-colored shoe. It looked to be a woman's slip on, like a ballet shoe, but the civilian version. I couldn't help but sigh because Forrest's big old feet wouldn't fit in those.

"This was left behind. I figured my mirror made them solid long enough for one of them to lose a shoe, then they took off." The old woman looked overtly proud.

Kudos to her. If I'd saved my friend from a shadow monster, I'd probably feel the same way. "May I see it?"

Her suspicious glare made my hand shake, but I kept it extended.

Tucker tilted his head at me but didn't offer his opinion. Good, because I felt the curiosity with my tightening gut and tingling fingers and didn't feel like explaining. It was better when we only interacted when I was drunk and we were naked. I couldn't handle one more truth.

But one more truth wasn't done with me yet. Having made her decision, Henrietta placed the shoe in my hand, but she held onto the heel. I was sure she was prepared to snatch it back if I got too possessive. Unfortunately, I felt nothing at all. No familiar sensation, no impression, nothing. It was just a shoe. I released my grip and Henrietta had the shoe hidden in her pull-string bag before I had the time to decide whether I was disappointed or relieved.

A voice on an intercom came from speakers all over the room, giving it an otherworldly feeling. "St. Benedict's closes in half an hour, please place your dinner trays in the proper receptacles, log off of any computer terminal, and remove your laundry from the cleaning room. Bagged meals are available for distribution at the exit. May God watch over you until we meet again."

The old woman crossed herself. "Amen."

Tucker helped her stand. "Are you okay for the night?"

She took out her mirror and held it to her chest. "I have a full belly, God, and this here mirror. I'm great." She started to shuffle toward the door, then turned around and gestured to me. "You should be careful though. I think the Shadows have their eye on you."

"I will?" What else could I say when all I wanted to do was run away from her creepy warning. When did I start living in a horror movie?

With his arm around my shoulder, Tucker pulled me in for another hug. "I'll be your mirror."

He kissed me on the top of my head in a way that was much more intimate than the dirty dancing we'd been practicing. My stomach tried to claw its way through my throat again, and I couldn't take another second.

Gina waved to us from the kitchen side of the counter. "Y'all ready for some dinner?"

I ran away from the successful, smart, kind, sexy doctor like he was one of Henrietta's Shadows. "I am starving, and I know there's a Happy Hour just around the corner with my name on it."

I felt Tucker's disappointment, but I didn't have the energy to coddle anyone or explain my ridiculous behavior. After a few drinks, I'd take him back to his place and make it up to him.

Twice if he's lucky.

Chapter Fifteen

Tucker's condo was spotless as always. I tossed my shoes haphazardly across the entryway to make it feel more lived in. My scarred foot only ached a bit at the movement. I wondered if it would ever not feel wrong.

Tucker had stopped right quick to check his mail since he hadn't been home in a couple days. Maybe that was how he kept this place so clean, just never came home. Well, I was glad I offered the overworked professional some motivation to make it back. Luckily, the fridge still had a few beers, though not much else. I needed to cook for him again.

By the time I had two beers opened and my shirt off, Tucker had made it up. His face flushed with heat as the mail was quickly forgotten and he pulled me against his firm chest. His warmth enveloped me at the same time as his lust tingled all the right spots. Since my empathy had gotten so much use today, I wondered how much of it would be on with Tucker tonight. Apparently, familiarity bred deeper connection because I could feel it all. The tequila from the Happy Hour margaritas that were too cheap to pass up blended with the bitter beer and loosened my barriers until everything was on fire in the best possible way.

Tucker's eyes were slitted and his voice heavy. "You're still overdressed."

What an invitation. I pushed him back reluctantly until he fell onto the foot of the bed. "Hey, Hottie, play 'Why don't you do right' by Jessica Rabbit." So I reprogrammed his device to respond to "Hey, Hottie." I thought it was funny.

With a swish of my hips and my modest chest pushed out as far as it would go, I started what I imagined to be an enticing strip tease. Considering Tucker's slack-jawed expression, it was pretty effective. My pants came off and cold air tickled my skin. I was so glad I shaved yesterday. Everything was smooth and ready for Tucker's attention.

As soon as I reached back to snap off my bra, my shoulder screamed at the angle. Lost in the moment, I'd forgotten what my body could do and what it couldn't. I'd never get back full movement. Hours of physical therapy only gave me about 75 percent. Suddenly, my scar seemed to glow, and I covered it with my good arm.

Before I fell into self-pity, the sultry voice of Jessica Rabbit and Tucker's emotional leap of sympathy hardened my core. Nope, that horrible man was not going to take my joy. If I said it often enough, I'd take my power back. At least that was what the Collected said. Besides, Tucker had seen it all since he was the admitting physician on duty when I was brought in. He never once showed any lack of attraction.

With my voice as low as it would go and still sound feminine, I said, "Time for the audience participation portion of tonight's performance."

I backed up into Tucker, grinding into his lap. For some reason, it felt dirtier with me almost naked and he still fully clothed. Without saying a word, Tucker unhooked my bra with one hand, while he reached around with his other and cupped my breast under the loosened bra. A fall of my shoulders let the bra cascade to the floor and freed Tucker's other hand to lean me back against him. When his lips found my neck, his lust jolted through every cell and merged with my own until even my lips were on fire and demanded to join with his.

With a gentle push on his knees, I lifted myself up and attempted to pivot. My foot, however, decided it had worked enough today and refused to hold my weight. As my ankle twisted and I collapsed, Tucker caught me before I unattractively smashed into the floor.

He picked me up with little effort and cradled me in his arms like we were posing for the cover of a cheesy romance. My head fell back as laughter gripped me. It was either that or cry, and I'd done enough of that for a lifetime.

Tucker's amusement tickled my fingers and toes, which just made me laugh harder. Until he bent down and took a nipple in his mouth. The shocking change in tone filled me with aching desire. I moaned and arched my back, forcing a tighter connection to his mouth. When he pulled away, a sigh of disappointment escaped my lips.

His eyebrow raised, obviously proud of himself. "That's better."

After tossing me on the bed and removing his shirt and pants in record time, Tucker crawled over me until his weight comforted me with its very presence. When his lips touched mine, need took over. My mind shut off and my senses opened, magnifying everything we felt until every caress was bliss.

Empathy was definitely a gift. And that night, I got to open it.

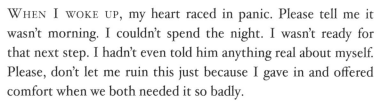

When I woke up, my heart raced in panic. Please tell me it wasn't morning. I couldn't spend the night. I wasn't ready for that next step. I hadn't even told him anything real about myself. Please, don't let me ruin this just because I gave in and offered comfort when we both needed it so badly.

With a curse directed at Tucker's blackout curtains, I clambered out of bed and searched for my phone. Now if I could sense where I put every damn thing I set down without thinking about it, that would be a useful skill. Beside the fridge, I finally located the cell that flashed 12 a.m. My tense muscles loosened, and my breathing calmed. I could sneak out of here and still get a nap in before heading back to the GRB with Amelia. Probably still too drunk to drive home, I scheduled an Uber and used the flashlight app to find my clothes. I thought I was clever tossing them all over until I stumbled around in the dark trying to locate all the pieces.

"You don't have to leave, you know." From the dark threshold of his bedroom, Tucker leaned against the door in the sexy way protagonists in YA romances always managed to squeeze into every movie.

"I have a long day tomorrow at the convention." Though that had nothing to do with why I had to go, at least it was something happening. The truth covering the lie made it easier to look him in the eye as my hand found the exit.

Tucker let out a deep breath. "I really like having you around and wonder what it would be like to wake up with you beside me."

The leg of my pants refused to cooperate as if they were conspiring with Tucker to keep me here. "I want to experience that too, but not tonight." I didn't have a good reason, so I left it at that and grabbed my phone and wallet.

Tucker stepped forward, still completely naked, and pinned me to the wall with his very presence. "Maybe you need more convincing."

Damn, how did he manage to smell so good after the sweating we just did? My free hand pet his chest, while my other clutched my phone and wallet. Half of me wanted to stay and the other half begged to flee. Through his skin, his doubt and frustration leaked into me. I closed my eyes to try to stop the twitching and rubbed my own chest to fight the hollow feeling.

No, I couldn't give in. Not yet. Maybe with more practice

with the Collected. Maybe if I could get my life in order and not fall apart at the slightest change in mood. For now, if I stayed, Tucker would see how fucked up I was. Even if he didn't know why, the signs and instability would be obvious. He already had to deal with my damaged body. Why would he choose to stay and deal with my damaged mind as well? By seeing each other a couple times a week, I seemed independent and in control and fascinating. I'd lose his interest or, worse, chase him away, if he saw what I was really like. I enjoyed my time with Tucker. No, I needed my time with Tucker so desperately, I wasn't willing to risk it by pushing our relationship forward too quickly.

"Tucker, I can't. Not yet." That was as honest as I could be.

The man of my dreams tightened his jaw and stepped back, staring at the floor the whole time. "As you wish."

My jaw mirrored his as sadness gripped me just as strongly. Refusing to touch him again in case I caved and fell into his arms, I scooted along the wall and opened the door.

He wasn't done with me yet though. "But so you're aware, this is not sustainable for me. I want more."

A tear trailed down my cheek as I thought to myself, *So do I.*

TRAFFIC WAS dead on the street in front of Tucker's building. It was Tuesday late, or maybe Wednesday really early depending on how you looked at it. All of the good boys and girls were at home sleeping, preparing for work the next day. Less than a year ago, I stood on this very spot and recognized the blue-trimmed condos just down the street. The moment I busted through Albert Johnson's door, the only other empath I'd ever found had been murdered and my entire life changed. After helping to solve his murder and catch the psychopath who hunted empaths, I'd grown more confident in my abilities, no longer considering them a curse. I'd used them to help solve cold cases and bring peace to a dozen victims' families. I found a group of people who could help me conquer my inability to function in crowds—or in life generally. My best friends in the world knew what I could do, and they didn't run away.

When the Uber arrived, I glanced up at Tucker's dark windows. Yet in some ways, I hadn't progressed at all. I still used alcohol as a crutch, and I still couldn't fully commit to the most incredible man I'd ever met. I wasn't even sure if I was more afraid of moving forward or losing him forever.

The older Indian driver didn't say a word as we passed a group of sleeping bags with humans likely curled up inside. I wondered how many had been at the rally the other night. Defeating the serial killer conquered my fear of my own ability. Maybe if I confronted my brother, I could heal the relationship part of me that was broken.

It was worth a try. Tucker was worth it. And maybe I was too.

Chapter Sixteen

My bra irritated me for some reason. I must have put it on backward or cockeyed or something after running from Tucker as quickly as I could. I had just made it home and was somehow too tired to make it all the way to the bedroom just another few steps away. Yet my brain wouldn't shut off so easily as I realized I'd signed myself up for a doozy again tomorrow.

First thing Wednesday morning, I'd attend the convention with Amelia, so I could convince some of the companies to donate to St. Benedict's. It was good publicity for a good cause and tax deductible. I was confident I could get a few to agree to open their wallets, enough to replace the ancient devices anyway. Improving the Wi-Fi was next. More of the people using the facility had cell phones than I had expected. A reliable Internet connection would go a long way.

Plus, after the reminder of all the shitty things I'd done to so many people over the years, it was time to give back.

After managing to remove my bra without unbuttoning my shirt, I laid down on the couch and pulled my grandmother's blanket over my shoulders. The happy hormones from great sex and the buzz of a few strong margaritas helped quiet the raging thoughts that had tormented me since I saw Forrest. Sleep would feel good.

NOT TWO MINUTES LATER, my phone rang. After fumbling with the blanket and my tangled clothes and my still sleeping reflexes, I managed to find my cell on the floor by the couch. The much too bright screen told me it was 7 a.m. as it flashed *Mateo Flores*.

Well, okay, much longer than two minutes then. Somehow the knowledge that I'd slept longer than I thought gave me a burst of energy. "What's up, Flores? Don't they let you sleep?"

The groan that escaped his lips made me picture him rubbing his chin as he was oft to do. "The precinct insists, but murderers don't comply with that ruling."

My flippancy hardened as I prepared myself for the news. "What happened?"

"It's another supposed suicide, but there's no weapon. It has all the markings of a pattern." He inhaled. "You've been invited if you want to give it a look."

"Where?"

"In front of St. Benedict's Homeless Initiative. Close to where the first body dropped."

Before I realized I'd moved, I had a cold coffee from the fridge and poured a touch of whiskey into it. "Seriously? I was just there yesterday."

I couldn't sense Flores's reaction over the phone, but I translated his "hmph" as, "You sure have a lot of connections to all of these murders. I'm going to have to add you to the suspect list. Too bad. I'll miss those cinnamon muffins you make for me." Of course, he didn't say any of this.

Instead, he sighed deeply. "I can send a patrol car to pick you up."

After downing at least half the glass of coffee, I answered, "Amelia will be here any minute to take me to the GRB for that tech convention. I can have her drop me off and meet up with her later."

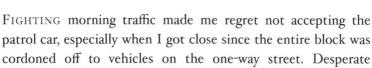

FIGHTING morning traffic made me regret not accepting the patrol car, especially when I got close since the entire block was cordoned off to vehicles on the one-way street. Desperate drivers late for work took chances they probably shouldn't to get into a turning lane. Most things about living in the city fit my vibe, but traffic could eat the big one.

I was glad Amelia drove and not me. She had her business face on and wouldn't let any nonsense from other drivers delay me. That allowed me time to put up my walls and prep for the scene.

When we were only a few steps away from the cordoned off section, I pointed to the sidewalk. "At this red light, I'll hop out. It will make an easy turn around spot for you."

Amelia nodded, but her concern filled the car. "Are you sure you don't want me to go with you?"

"Even if I did, I don't think they'd let you on the scene." I clipped my special consultant badge to the lapel of my jacket. "I'll find my way to the convention after we're done here." *If I have the energy to keep it all up*, I wanted to add.

Amelia smiled. "I hope so."

She pulled up to the red light, and I jumped out before anyone had time to get annoyed. The crowd was pretty thick on the sidewalk, and they vibrated a mix of frustration and curiosity. The sensations moved from one bit of my body to another. Across the street, I flashed my badge at the uniformed officer directing people away. He waved me through before having to argue with another gentleman in a three-piece suit that he was just going to have to go around. I did not envy the officer his job. Then again, maybe he didn't envy me mine.

Since Flores's personality, quiet but in command, seemed to

take up so much space, I was always surprised when I couldn't spot him immediately. His height put him at a disadvantage for spotting in a crowd. The same couldn't be said for Collins who saw me at the same time as I saw him. His bullish build walked through, rather than around, the other officers to get to me. My stomach clenched so viciously, it felt like I'd been stabbed again.

Collins wasn't upset. He was truly pissed. Judging by the dark look in his eyes, it was all aimed at me. "I knew you were a con artist. I knew it from the moment I laid eyes on you. I want you to know that if you do anything to hurt Flores, I will make you pay."

With my jaw locked into place due to his severe emotional reaction, I couldn't reply. I have no doubt my wide-eyed fear and shaky head nod made Collins know I understood.

He straightened his back giving my lungs room to breathe and my stomach distance to untie a knot or two. I had no intention of hurting anyone ever again, but there was no way I could prove that to this man who had been against me from the beginning. I learned early on which people would serve as marks and which wouldn't. Even on the worst days, Forrest and I would have stayed clear of someone like Collins. If only I had that luxury now.

Flores's voice called from down the street. "Fauna, is that you?"

I resisted sprinting around the much larger detective to get to the safe vicinity of Flores. As I side-stepped gently to the right, Collins opened his arm as if welcoming me to the scene. Well, he had welcomed me, but I wouldn't call it a warm one.

The *clip clap* of my professional flats echoed on the concrete. I concentrated on the rhythm trying to center myself before having to give Flores a reading. My mother's voice sang in my head. Though it had proven to not be the best barrier against the outside world—which was why it didn't work so well for most of my life—I still couldn't help but make it the first step in my process.

The short detective stood a few feet from the sheet-covered body of the victim. "I'm sorry to interrupt your plans. I know you didn't find anything at the Remington estate, but I hoped maybe a fresh scene would give more information."

"It usually does. Everything is still raw and upfront." Which was exactly how I was feeling at the moment. "Am I allowed to touch the, uh, person?" He hadn't given me any details on what had happened.

He held up a pair of blue plastic gloves. "As long as you wear these."

I answered the question his raised eyebrows asked, "They're pretty thin. I can make it work."

As I struggled to squeeze my sweaty fingers into the latex, Flores motioned for the crime scene techs to lift the sheet. With my focus on the gloves, I used my mom's hymn to reinforce the barrier I'd learned to construct, the separation between my authentic self and another's thoughts. A crack sliced the wall in half as soon as I saw the face of the victim. It was Henrietta, the old woman from St. Benedict's who warned Tucker and I about the shadows. Her skin had gone ashy, and her clothes were half soaked in her own blood. A quick glance at her sliced wrists, showed the jagged lines Flores spoke of with the other victims. The wound looked torn more than sliced cleanly. Yet, if she'd done this herself, why did she lay so peacefully with a look of complete calm on her face? And why couldn't they find a tool that would make those marks at the scene?

Did the Shadows get her? Maybe I should have believed her. After so much of my life involved no one believing me, why did I do the same to her? Maybe somebody else saw what she had with Xavier. But she'd said the Shadows caused the Wasting, not that they murdered people. I turned to Flores. "Were there any witnesses?"

Flores rubbed his chin, the uncharacteristic stubble proof of his lack of sleep. "If you can call them that. Each of them spoke of—"

I interrupted him, "Shadows."

He took a minute to study me with his thick eyebrows shielding his eyes. "How did you know that?" he asked.

I couldn't feel anything from him and wasn't sure if I should approach the poor woman now that I'd confessed to our connection. But I wasn't about to leave anything out for the rest of this case. If Flores stopped trusting me, I wasn't sure how I'd move forward. For some reason, I needed his approval. "I met her yesterday at St. Benedict's. Henrietta is her name and she said she saw Shadows approach Xavier, another homeless man, before he fell ill. I have no idea what she really saw, but she was telling the truth, at least from her perspective. I've seen so many unexplained things lately, I don't know what to make of any of it."

Flores thumbed notes into his cell. "Yes, there have been quite a few unexplainable things lately."

I felt Collins behind me even though I didn't turn around. His anger was starting to be a familiar signature. It was like he wasn't just angry with me but with the world. "So you knew this victim too? What did you con her out of?"

"I didn't ..." Thinking of Collins's living impression reminded me of the familiar one. I loosened my barriers a bit and walked around the body, careful not to impact the scene. "Gina and I were volunteering at St. Benedict's and Henrietta was there. That's my only connection."

I knew he must have heard me tell Flores but repeating myself bought me some time to do a full circumference. And there it was, enveloping a parking meter like an old plastic bag waving in the wind. My whole being told me I knew who this was. I had to learn more. I needed to touch Henrietta to see if I could get anything from the contact. Why would Flores keep me around if I never discovered anything interesting? The recent successes with the cold cases didn't seem as important as what was happening now.

Collins crossed his arms and stared down at me from his full height. "You seem to be—"

Flores stopped him with a touch on his elbow. "Not now Collins. You and I can discuss it later." His soulful gaze and encouraging nod gave me all the confidence I needed to continue.

After crouching down in an area by her shoulder relatively free of blood, I put a gentle hand on her cheek. I felt nothing. It was weird to touch a human being and not feel a thing. That's what a peaceful death felt like to me, a stripping of the human essence from the flesh. But how could she have been at peace and then died this way? It was more like a reflection of Henrietta, like whatever it was that made up this unique individual had been stripped away and sent to the other side of the looking glass. Or maybe I read *Alice in Wonderland* one too many times growing up.

Then I realized what I was missing. Where was her mirror? I flicked back the sheet a bit more to see her waist where there was no sign of her drawstring bag.

Flores crouched down beside me. "What is it?"

My face scrunched from my own confusion. "When we spoke with Henrietta, she used a mirror to chase away the Shadows. She kept it in a drawstring bag."

Flores waved over a tech. "Officer Pradock, have you found a drawstring bag while looking for a blade?"

I recognized Officer Pradock immediately as the one who took blood samples from my hands on the day I found Albert Johnson murdered in his apartment. He looked just as exhausted as he had then.

He didn't pay me any attention, but he did wave at Flores to follow him. "We found one in the dumpster."

Not wanting to be left alone with Collins, I followed Flores and Pradock around the corner. A tech covered in a protective suit, and not so quietly cursing the short straw she drew, pulled things from a dumpster.

Officer Pradock pointed to an evidence bag containing the same drawstring purse I remembered from yesterday. When I bent down to see if I could see a mirror handle, that familiar signature emanated from it. Yesterday, the signature wasn't there, I'd checked. This had to be fresh, new. Had my brother been down here? Was Henrietta part of his scheme somehow? Someone had to drum up the homeless to attend his rallies.

One way or another, there was one thing I couldn't deny. "It's the same person involved in all three suicides. There's something here, but not my usual ..." The other techs stared at me and my mouth clenched shut. I didn't need to clarify in public. Flores knew what I meant. I stood with my hands on my hips. "Was anything missing from the other victims?"

Flores shook his head but checked his notes anyway. "Nothing reported as missing. It was how we knew it wasn't a robbery made to look like a suicide." He followed straight to where I was heading. "So why did the person responsible take the valueless bag from a homeless woman and throw it away nearby?"

I thought I knew why. They'd left evidence, and Henrietta had found it. "The shoe. Henrietta also kept a shoe in that bag she said the Shadows dropped when she chased them away."

After receiving a nod of approval from Flores, Pradock waved over a photographer. "Take pictures of everything as I lay it out."

Pradock pulled one piece at a time from the bag, calling what he found as he went. "Neatly folded but empty potato chip bag. A plastic, beaded child's barrette. A gold band, maybe a wedding ring? A belled cat collar. And a cracked vanity mirror. That's it."

"Henrietta must not have seen them coming. She didn't have time to grab her mirror. But where is the shoe?"

Flores turned his curiosity on me. "What did it look like?"

"It was a blush-colored slip-on." The confusion on Flores's face was obvious without getting close enough to feel it. "It looks kind of like a ballet slipper, but it's more comfortable and casual."

His thumbs flew over his screen. "So Shadows wear shoes now?"

"Exactly. It's nuts, right?" The term made me feel guilty. Who was I to judge another's mental state. "Maybe she actually saw the murderer and that sighting made her think of Shadows or maybe it was too dark to see anything or ..."

He paused in his note taking. "Which would mean that shoe could have belonged to another witness."

It was my turn to look quizzical. "I mean, at least a person of interest."

"You need to stop watching crime procedurals." Flores shook his head as he addressed Pradock, "Search the area again for the shoe she described."

I ripped a glove off one hand and found a similar style on my phone as a reference for Pradock. When I dropped the blue vinyl in the evidence ring, Pradock's thankful look turned to exhausted disappointment.

"I'm sorry. I didn't mean to," I mumbled.

In my awkward bend to pick it up while not touching any other bit of evidence, my dress flats slipped in something unidentifiable on the ground. Adrenaline flooded my panicked mind. Pinwheeling my arms as if I had any sense of how to redirect my momentum, I ended up hopping over a to-go container. Before I plummeted to the ground, I grabbed the dumpster for stabilization.

As soon as I touched it, I almost vomited. An impression I hadn't suspected was there. It yanked me from the morning sun and dropped me into the dead of night. My stomach tried to empty in front of the dumpster as the person who left the memory had. I resisted the urge to release the metal and back off. I hadn't seen anything useful yet. Maybe this could help.

I focused on riding the memory instead of participating. I could do this. I'd been practicing. Judging by the men's Nikes and cargo pants, I could guess the gender of the memory leaver. They were both pretty clean for someone who lived on the street. Either they were new or it wasn't a homeless person.

Then he spoke. "Michelle, oh my God, don't look over there. There's a dead body."

It was my brother. I was inside an impression he left behind. It was him. The impossible was true. Forrest was the murderer.

Chapter Seventeen

The shock of the true character of my brother froze me. I couldn't remove my hand from the source. I had to see it through.

Michelle's petite form materialized beside the dark dumpster like she'd been hiding in the shadow. That must be what Henrietta saw. There was so much shadow from the streetlights and still lit buildings, anything could be hiding in their depths. But why would Michelle and Forrest be down here? Maybe Michelle was the one. It could be her I'm sensing, right? At this point, any straws I could grab I reached for.

Michelle tucked something into her back pocket as she walked to Forrest. "The streets are dangerous. We shouldn't even be out here. I warned you."

"I know. I know. But there's no other way."

All I got from Forrest was fear and disgust. No murderous intent. No satisfaction from a fresh kill. No guilt over what he might have just done. That might have been the most surreal bit of this experience. I couldn't feel my brother's feelings at all in person. It was nice to know that he did truly possess some.

Michelle scoffed as she checked out something on the other

side of the dumpster. "I told you I could find another way if you gave me time. I'm the only one who has never left you."

After wiping his mouth, Forrest joined Michelle on the other side of the dumpster. Through his eyes, I saw Heidi laying prone on the ground beside a coughing man dressed in clothes as oil stained as the street underneath him. When I sucked in a shocking breath, I almost choked on the fumes from the slowly warming metal garbage container. I yanked my hand from the impression before it repeated.

Flores had a hand on my elbow guiding me from the cordoned off area before I realized I'd moved. "What did you see?" He spoke quietly, but it didn't matter. I couldn't care less what anyone else thought as my world slowly fell apart. Whether it was Forrest or Michelle I sensed, he was still running the show; it was his fault regardless. How could he condone murder?

While the images flashed in my brain and I tried to realign my world, Pradock waved an evidence bag and a pair of temp shoes like the ones from the nail salon when you forgot to wear toeless shoes to the appointment. That was when I realized I'd slipped in some of my brothers vomit when I grabbed the dumpster for support. Ironically, I might never have found the impression if Forrest didn't have such a weak stomach. Flores helped balance me as I switched my shoes out and tried to ignore Pradock's disappointed expression.

The pause in questioning allowed my brain to focus on what was missing from the scene. "Let me check something?" I requested more than ordered. I couldn't tell if Heidi was alive or dead in the vision. I had to know if she still laid in the alley, another victim of my brother.

Apparently, I hadn't destroyed all of my good will with Flores. He let go of my arm and let me take the lead. I rushed to where I'd seen Heidi in the image. A crooked tower of cardboard leaned precariously against the chipped paint of the metal. I pushed it over with my foot, unwilling to dive into any other emotion.

Pradock expressed the most emotion I'd ever seen from him. "We hadn't gotten to that side yet. How will I document it now?"

Nothing was revealed, but I still couldn't see the ground. She and the homeless man could still be under there. There was no pile of cardboard in my vision.

Before I completely lost it, I asked Flores for help. "I have to know what's underneath. I think it's vitally important."

Flores's forehead crinkled as he pointed at something within the tumbled pile. "Is that a foot?"

Oh god, oh god, please don't let it be Heidi. I should have grabbed her and ran away when I first saw her with Forrest. While I scooted back to give the techs room to move the cardboard much more carefully than I had, Flores called out to the prone body hidden underneath.

"Are you awake in there? Can you hear me?"

Collins pulled up beside me, but I was too distraught to feel annoyed. "What have you done to him now?"

Well, I supposed there was room for a little annoyance. "Are you serious? There's another victim under there, and you think I did something to Flores."

As the pile cleared, I didn't see two pairs of feet like in the memory. I rubbed my head to clear the vision and the feeling of disgust from my brother or maybe it was my own disgust at him.

Pradock shot up from the ground. "He's alive. Manners, order an ambulance now."

Unable to take comfort from the masculine pronoun, I rushed beside Flores. "Keep looking. There could be another victim."

Flores pulled me aside. His intense stare made it impossible for me to avoid his question. "What did you see?"

It was time anyway. Why did I live a life where I always had to confess? "It was my brother, Forrest. He was here. I don't know when, but he threw up by the dumpster because he'd seen a dead body. So I'm assuming—"

"It was last night." Flores rubbed the shadow of a beard on his chin. "We did take a sample of vomit but had no idea if it was connected or just a random drunk, but it was definitely fresh."

Collins folded his arms, but I could see his hands shake with rage even as it made my jaw ache. "Your brother was also connected with Sylvia Remington."

There was no denying it. I watched Flores and Collins put together the pieces just like I had. "But he wasn't connected to the first victim. My brother wouldn't kill anyone. Why would he lose it when he saw a dead body if he was killing them?" I guess I still had it in me to defend him. Though I didn't think I convinced anyone, least of all myself.

Collins waved his arm around the alley. "Well, if he was here, it's only a street away from the volunteer."

Flores didn't radiate any emotion at all. I had no idea what he was thinking. "Do you know where he is?"

No time for lying. I guess we'd find out together. "No, but I did see him yesterday." A tear dripped down my cheek, and I rubbed it on my shoulder. This was not the time to show weakness, not with Collins watching everything I did.

"Family can be difficult." Flores stared at the ground.

Pradock interrupted our arguing to address Flores. "Detective, there's no sign of external injury. The man under the cardboard is just really sick."

Collins almost looked disappointed. "So not another victim."

The tech signed something handed to him after giving it a quick glance. "The EMTs say whatever it is, it's been running through the homeless community."

"The Wasting," I said.

Collins and Flores both looked at me.

"That's what they're calling it. Tucker, er, Dr. Wickman said he's seen multiple cases throughout the city, all among the homeless."

"Well, a sickness isn't under my banner of responsibility." After taking one deep breath that seemed to last a lifetime,

Flores said, "Let's go find your brother and see where that leads."

Resisting the urge to fling my arms around his neck in a hug, I simply nodded in agreement.

When Collins tried to lean in, Flores held a hand up to keep him back. "Will you finish at the scene? Fauna and I have some interviews to conduct."

The older detective straightened. My jaw tightened again at his seething anger. I thought he was much calmer when we first met. I was not normally such a bad judge of character, given what I could do. I wondered what happened recently to make him so much more protective of his partner. From what I'd seen so far, Flores could take care of himself.

When Collins didn't offer an objection, Flores indicated his Ford Fusion parked partially on the sidewalk. "Lead the way."

"Behind the GRB is where I saw him last." I pulled my gloves out of my bag. Progress or no, I felt extra vulnerable to introduce my brother to my new friend who thought I was awesome. "So you're aware, I can't sense my brother's emotions like I can most people."

"Well, I've been doing this a long time without being able to sense anyone's emotions." Flores pulled into traffic without having to use his lights. "We'll manage."

As we weaved around the traffic caused by the morning commute and the closed lanes, I tried to decide what I'd do when we ran into my brother. A mix of emotions swam through me. My brother wasn't a murderer; he couldn't be.

Flores stared out the window, but I felt his turmoil in the air. "So you can't read your own family? After all the things I've seen you do, that surprises me."

Did he think I was lying so I wouldn't have to finger my own brother? "I can read my family. Sparrow is an open book. You could probably read him. My mother's emotions were always crystal clear. She was constantly afraid, like a cloak she drug with her everywhere we went. Gina, Amelia, you."

Though he tilted his head when I put him in the category of family, Flores didn't say anything.

"It's just Forrest I can't read. Neither of us know why."

"What about your father?" Flores asked without taking his eyes off the road.

I resisted the urge to pull my knees up and hug them. "He died when I was pretty young. I have no idea."

Accompanied by Flores's lifted eyebrows and softened lips, a wave of deep sorrow washed over me, almost making me cry. "I'm sorry, Fauna."

"It was a long time ago, but it is why Forrest and I had such a strained relationship. He tried to be the man of the household even though there was no household."

When we arrived at the once-abandoned block, there were so many people milling about, there was little room to park. The RV was still there, but the stage had grown and included lighting somehow. In the parking spot we pulled into, a few higher-class cars took up other spaces. Their owners remained inside instead of mixing with the mostly homeless population outside: desperate enough to take a chance with a traveling healer but not desperate enough to risk exposure to people below their class. It kind of upset my stomach, but I knew the truly wealthy clients wouldn't come at all. Forrest liked house calls.

After putting the car into park, Flores looked me in the eye. "I can do this on my own. You don't have to come."

My head shook back and forth pulled by my frowning lips. "This is my mess too. It needs to end."

Flores accepted my answer without vocalizing anymore doubt.

Though I did my best to not touch anyone, each individual spike of emotion stabbed my psyche like the rocks in the rough paved lot stabbed the bottoms of my feet through the thin temporary shoes. The overall emotion of the gathered was identical to the other day even though no one was on the stage. This must be how cults spread: a certain state of mind multiplied in the believers until others started to feel the same. Maybe more people were empaths even if they didn't have my extreme version.

"That's it." I indicated the modest RV. "After performing Monday, they retired into the RV."

Flores had a healthy dose of intuition at the very least, which he proved as he walked slightly in front of me and made a path. This must be how celebrities felt.

My momentary glow of importance faded as I thought of confronting my brother in front of all these people. I froze in front of the torn screen in the RV door. My feet refused to move closer, and my hands refused to clench into knocking fists.

With his head cocked at me, Flores leaned forward and knocked on the metal frame of the screen door. "Houston PD, can I come in and ask you a few questions?"

A loud thump shook the vehicle. Flores threw a protective arm in front of me while his other arm pushed his jacket aside for easy access to his firearm.

"No!" someone shouted from inside accompanied by more creaking.

Flores motioned for me to stand back, and he swung the screen door open. "Is everyone okay in there? Houston PD. I'm coming in if I feel someone is in trouble."

"Stop. You won't fit, you moron." That was Michelle, and she didn't sound distressed at all.

Before this got out of hand, I had to make myself known. "Forrest, it's me. We need to talk."

Immediately, the door swung open revealing my brother. Taller than me with the same shade of dirty blonde hair and the same slightly upturned nose, he hadn't seemed to age at all. "Fauna? I wondered if you'd come back to see me." Even the cadence of his voice matched mine. No matter how much I wanted to deny it, we were obviously related.

Michelle pulled someone out of the modest window over the tiny dining table. "Seriously, dude. I'm not cutting you out."

The man tumbled from the window, landing awkwardly on the cushioned bench seat. "Fauna Young?" Austin's messed up hair matched his confused expression.

"Hey." I found myself miffed about him being here and pushed past Forrest to get inside. "You promised you'd let me check it out first."

Austin slumped like a two-year-old caught with daddy's secret stash of candy bars. "I didn't hear from you at all yesterday, and we needed help now."

My jaw locked shut as Flores's anger overtook any other emotion in the modest RV. He practically growled at his husband. "What are you doing here?"

Chapter Eighteen

The calmness in the air of the RV surprised me, for I'd expected to feel that same familiar aura I'd experienced at multiple locations. Did that mean it wasn't Forrest or Michelle? But why then was it so familiar?

Before I could fully analyze what it all meant, Austin tore into me. "Why did you bring him here? I was setting up a meeting for Heidi to visit the prison without him even knowing. Now you've ruined it."

Did he say the prison? The person Flores had asked me to read was his cousin? I lifted an eyebrow at him. I guessed I wasn't the only one with deep-seeded family issues.

Austin's face was twisted in fury, but the stone in the pit of my stomach told me he was actually terrified. One family issue at a time.

I waved my hands in innocence at Austin. "I didn't bring Flores here to find you. I didn't even know you were here."

As Austin's cheeks flushed bright red, I saw something I never thought I'd experience. Flores lost it.

"What are you talking about? Why would you set up a meeting with anyone to visit Pedro? There's nothing to be done. A con artist isn't going to solve the problem or erase my guilt."

As if he suddenly remembered they weren't the only two people in the room, Flores stopped talking and took a deep breath. "We can talk about this at home."

While the experienced detective took in the rest of his surroundings, I followed his focus around the modest RV.

On the couch-like chair across from the mini-kitchen sat Heidi. Relief eased some of my tension since I hadn't known for sure she was okay until that moment. Michelle closed the creaky window over the kitchen sink facing the back of the parking lot. Austin pulled on his wrinkled shirt that looked so out of place when he was normally completely put together. I felt sorry for Austin. He was trying to help Flores but was going about it totally wrong.

Heidi's voice sounded so delicate after the angry men. "What do you mean con artist?"

Forrest obviously couldn't take not being the center of attention. He embraced me like we had any relationship left at all. Nevertheless, his warmth somehow brought me comfort.

Fuck him. That was how he always got to me. It was almost impossible to deny your older brother who fed you for years when your mother could barely function. It felt so odd to feel his heartbeat and his breath on the back of my neck but no hint of emotion at all. Maybe that's why I was getting this signature instead. Maybe he left stuff behind instead of carrying it with him? But if that were true, why didn't I sense any of it here?

Regardless, I couldn't accuse him of what I needed to accuse him of if I was stuck in his embrace. With a firm push, I made him back off. "You promised never to come back to Houston. What are you doing here?"

Forrest sat next to Heidi and put a comforting arm around her shoulder. "We're just passing through. I thought I'd be in and out before you noticed."

Michelle crossed her arms, her anger tensing my jaw. "We have important work to do here. And you don't own the city."

At least I knew where she stood. "Oh, yes, very important. I spotted the Lexus and brand-new BMW in the parking lot. And I saw how Forrest had a fit when Heidi chose a poor child to heal the other day."

Damn, I'd called her a healer out loud. I had to admit I couldn't figure out what I'd felt the other day when I'd witnessed the event. And who the hell was I to deny some sort of unexplainable ability when I myself had a few of those?

At a cough from Flores, I remembered I should probably formally introduce him. "Detective Flores, this is my brother Forrest and an old friend Michelle."

He nodded at both of them, then focused on Heidi. "And you are?"

Austin partially blocked the healer from Flores's scrutiny. "She's Heidi and she's a miracle who I've witnessed personally healing the ill. I heard you're skeptical about such things and only believe peer-reviewed evidence, but she's the real thing. And I know she can help your cousin."

Heat flashed across Flores's face. "Austin, this is police business and I'd appreciate it if you'd step outside."

Austin's strong jaw dropped, and his eyes blinked multiple times. Then he closed upon himself with his arms crossed and his hip cocked. He gestured to me. "Why does she get to stay?"

"Fauna has some inside knowledge." Dismissing the complaints of his husband, Flores stared at Forrest who seemed uncomfortable for the first time since we'd entered.

"Fine." Austin pushed by me a bit more aggressively than was necessary as he exited. What he portrayed as anger was actually fear and frustration that rubbed off on me as he brushed by. I hoped my family drama didn't hurt Austin and Flores's relationship. They were the most stable and happy couple I'd ever met, including Gina's parents. I didn't think I could stand it if something happened to break them up.

Forrest leaned forward to appear welcoming and open. Boy, was he in for a surprise. Flores didn't fall for such moves. "How can we help you, Detective? We've got an audience gathering outside who need the Healer."

His calm voice while the people around him suffered brought up my perpetual anger at him. The urge to shake Heidi's hand became overwhelming. "I'd love to meet the healer, personally. Are we only going to talk about her like she's not in the room?"

Forrest put a protective hand on Heidi's shoulder. What was he shielding her from? "She doesn't like to be touched by strangers. I would think you of all people would understand that."

That son of a bitch. How dare he try to spark my sympathy when he knew damn well he used me to line his pockets by making me touch all kinds of strangers. If anything, his statement made me want to get Heidi out of there more. "I might understand more than she does."

Red flushed across Forrest's face. Good. He was afraid of what I knew. If he'd been killing people to cover up his tracks, then he better be scared.

Though his head slanted down and he casually leaned against the kitchen counter like he wasn't paying any attention, Flores's eyes slanted upward giving me the confidence to push even more.

"I'd like to talk to Heidi myself as one former partner to another."

Heidi looked directly at me for the first time. "I thought you were his sister."

Energy swelled around her. Judging by the reaction of my body, it was mostly stress. I couldn't tell if the source was unfounded jealousy or hope that I could free her or something else entirely. But I did believe she'd talk to me if we were alone.

"I am Forrest's sister. I also used to travel with him and entertain large crowds, just like you're doing now."

Forrest became defensive. "And you earned a lot of money while we did. You chose to leave." He squeezed Heidi's shoulder tighter as if he couldn't lose his meal ticket. Not again anyway.

"We're not doing anything wrong, and we're not obligated to answer any question unless you're arresting us and then we'll just talk to our lawyer."

It was time for Flores to switch into his business mode. "I was curious about the permits for your informal gatherings. I'm assuming you have them."

Michelle pushed past us toward the door. "We most certainly do. They're in my car outside and are posted at every event. We have three more nights before we have to renew or move on."

Flores followed her but turned back for Forrest. "You've already said this was your show. I need to see your ID and make sure everything is legit."

Forrest's forehead crinkled with his frustration. It was weird to watch emotions on a person's face instead of feeling them. It was like watching a movie and made the whole scene less real. It had been so long since I'd hung with Forrest, I'd forgotten that part. As many times as I'd wished to not have this ability, life would be less real without it.

Forrest released Heidi but didn't take a single step away. "Fauna said I was her brother. Is her word not sufficient?"

Man, he really didn't want to leave Heidi with me. That made me want to be alone with her even more. The abuser always separated their victim from everyone to keep them under control. If Heidi wanted out, I'd give her the chance.

Flores countered, "She's a civilian and I need something more official to write on the paperwork, especial if I need to make an arrest for lack of cooperation."

One thing had to be said for Forrest: he knew when he'd been out maneuvered. He always knew when it was time to leave town. "Fine. Heidi, get your shoes and let's go."

The air seemed to thicken as Heidi straightened her back and looked my brother straight in the eye. "I think I'll stay and talk to Fauna."

Forrest shook his head but didn't say another word. Instead, he followed Michelle out the door. Flores gave me a questioning look.

"I'm good," I said out loud, then mouthed at him, *Thank you.*

He shrugged and closed the door behind him.

Heidi looked up at me. "You traveled with Forrest before? He never talks of you. It would have been nice to have someone to call to figure out how to deal with all of this."

She seemed so sweet. Either I was taken in by her like so many of the fans outside or she really was that innocent. I suppose there was only one way to find out. "I'm afraid I never learned to deal with the crowd and Forrest's demands. But if you need out, I'm here for you." I dropped down on the sofa next to her and touched her hand lightly.

My body vibrated with power, like I'd been shocked by an electrical wire. "Holy shit."

Chapter Nineteen

With a yank, Heidi pulled her arm away and jumped up from the couch. "I'm sorry. I wasn't ready for a touch. I have a ritual to prepare myself for helping people and you came in before I'd started it."

Interesting. "But you touched Forrest, or rather he touched you, without any difficulty?"

Heidi blushed like I'd just caught her in bed with my brother. "My ability doesn't work on him for some reason. He's always safe to touch."

Even more interesting. This might say more about Forrest than it did either of us. "You know, my empathic ability doesn't work on him either. I could never get a reading. Maybe Forrest's power is the ability to resist us."

After shaking out her arms, she seemed to calm down enough to sit beside me, though she tucked her hands between her legs and leaned away. "Maybe. I hadn't thought about it. Because he's able to help me recover faster than I've ever been able to."

"Recover?" Sitting this close, I could feel her turmoil almost as strongly as if I'd touched her directly.

Before she began, Heidi closed her eyes as if to gather her

thoughts. Then again, maybe she was deciding on whether she should confide in me or not. Heaven only knew what Forrest had told her about me. Luckily, she opened up as her energy seemed to settle on a decision, which was a relief to my crawling skin.

"After I heal a client, I'm weak. It's not like that Star Trek episode where the alien girl heals the humans and takes on the exact symptoms the sick person had."

The title to the show popped up in my head and I couldn't help but appreciate the irony. "'The Empath.' I remember that one."

Heidi smiled weakly. "Forrest must have made you watch all those old things too."

For some reason, the nostalgia lightened my anger. The emotion surprised me. "Actually, I made him watch them. They were always on after school and brought me comfort while he was working and Mom napped."

"Huh, I just assumed." Heidi blinked and leaned a little closer to me. "Anyway, I don't get their disease or injury. But something is drained in me like I completed a marathon and forgot to carb load first. Before Forrest, I'd recover over many days of rest. It made holding any sort of job temporary and with no support system at home, I struggled."

At that moment, I realized I believed Heidi. She was the real deal. "These gifts don't make normal life easy."

She laughed, a light-hearted, beautiful twittering. "That's putting it mildly."

The urge to invite her into the Collected had my foot tapping. I couldn't. It was my safe place, and I didn't want Forrest anywhere near it. Maybe if I got her away from him. "So how did Forrest con you into touring with him and healing all of these strangers?"

"He didn't con me." Heidi crossed her arms as her anger made my jaw clench. "Forrest showed me the ability to heal wasn't a curse, but a gift I could use to improve the lives of others."

"For a price." I felt like a parent telling their child there was no Santa Claus. After all, Forrest never helped me see my ability as any more than a useful curse.

Heidi shook her head and leaned away. "We have to eat and put gas in the RV. I can't help anyone if we can't get to them."

I was losing her. I had to put away my bitterness and solve the mystery. I had to know if Heidi knew if Forrest was killing people. My entire being baulked at the very idea, but I couldn't deny his presence at every scene. Even though it didn't permeate the RV, nothing else made sense. Since I couldn't read him, maybe it was how my ability identified him in my memory? Maybe he only left the signature somewhere he hurt someone? Who did he hurt outside of the GRB when I felt it on the lamp post? One problem at a time.

Luckily, Heidi didn't sense my inner turmoil, or she didn't care, because she continued her defense of Forrest. "We met on accident. I was walking home from work when I saw a man bleeding in the street. He looked right at me and begged me to call an ambulance. There was so much blood running down the side of his face, I didn't know if an ambulance would be on time. I also hadn't healed anyone in weeks so I was at full power."

"So you healed him and he discovered your power and latched on."

She looked out the window, putting aside her anger much easier than I could. "No. I mean, I tried, but as I said earlier. My power doesn't work on him, which had never happened to me before. At first, I was relieved. Maybe it had worn out, like I only had a certain amount stored and once it was used, I was free to live a normal life. But I didn't have time to dwell on it because I had to get him help. That's when Michelle showed up."

That was puzzling. If Michelle had been nearby, why would Forrest be alone in the street bleeding? She'd always been attached to him like the typical unrequited love you see in teen movies, except there was no happy ending for her. She'd always treated me so poorly, I didn't feel sorry for her though.

Heidi didn't seem to notice my surprise and just kept telling the story. "We managed to get Forrest to a local ER where they patched up his head. Michelle tried to get me to leave multiple times, but Forrest insisted I stay. He said I was his good luck charm. If I hadn't found him, he might have bled out."

Sure he would have. "Did he say what happened?"

"He slipped and fell while looking at the map on his phone."

He always did have an answer for everything. Forrest would never have been that clumsy or that unprepared. He memorized the area we'd go to including the important buildings like the local police station and the exit routes if things turned sour—when things turned sour. So he was setting her up. But for what?

She kept speeding up like she'd never told anyone before, which she probably hadn't. "While Michelle and Forrest fought, I stepped into the hallway to give them privacy. A woman was rushed by me in a stretcher mumbling that it couldn't happen again, she couldn't lose another one. I noticed her swollen belly before they swished closed the privacy curtains."

That was when I realized her ability was much more powerful and much more devastating than mine. How do you see sick people all day and not heal every one of them? You would die, so of course you don't, but seeing torment you knew you could cure had to be much more curse-like than gift-like. "She was having a miscarriage?"

"That was my guess." Heidi let the tears rush down her face. "I'd experienced four when we were trying to have a baby in my first marriage. Imagine the person who could cure a complete stranger of any disease or illness but couldn't save her own babies."

Her water-filled eyes met mine and my body filled with her grief. Unfortunately, I could only share, not heal her pain. I leaned forward and put my hand close to her leg but didn't touch her. "I'm so sorry." It sounded pathetic, but I didn't know what else to say.

Heidi shook her head and cleared her throat. "It was a long

time ago, but I couldn't just stand there and let that poor woman suffer when I *could* save her baby. Yet, I couldn't figure out how to get past the nurses to see her. I had to touch her to make it happen. The thought of my failure with Forrest terrified me, but I knew I had to try. What was the point of all of those years of suffering if I couldn't help someone?"

Man, did I understand that sentiment. "What did you do?"

"Forrest came up behind me and put a hand on my shoulder. Something about his presence gave me strength. Without saying a word or preparing me at all, he guided me toward the distressed woman. He boldly told the attending that I was her sister and had to get in there. The poor young doctor seemed so overwhelmed he didn't argue.

"The pregnant woman doubled up in pain on the bed reminding me of my experience. I asked her to let me help. She said anything to save her baby. I put my hands on her abdomen and, like it always does, the healing took over, like it's a separate entity living in my body waiting to do this one deed. Energy poured from my fingers into her. At that time in my life, I had no control at all. The healing just did its thing and used me as a battery source.

"I watched her relax as I fell to my knees, too weak to stand anymore, but I still didn't let go. I had to be sure. When I was too weak to hold my hands against her skin, I collapsed, but Forrest caught me. He moved me aside as doctors rushed in to monitor the pregnant woman. Their looks of surprise as they comforted the woman and told her the baby's heartbeat was strong and her bleeding had stopped, that everything looked fine, was the only reward I needed."

Her hands shook as she studied them like they were someone else's. "I'd never used that much power before. It scared me when I realized Forrest still held me and I didn't want my body to absorb his strength to replace my own. With a rush of adrenaline, I pushed him off and yelled at him not to touch me, but I didn't have the strength to move from the floor. Your brother surprised me when he explained my power didn't work on him, so he could safely move me. And he did. Michelle came out of nowhere with a wheelchair that Forrest put me in and out we went. In the car, I explained that if I touched anyone—except Forrest it seemed—I would heal them, but if I was weak, then the healing would recharge my batteries with the other person's strength. My strength would rebound on its own but it took time. Sometimes days. Forrest assured me he'd dealt with people with powers before," she gestured toward me, "and would be able to help me heal faster.

"When I woke up the next morning, I was at full strength. I questioned Forrest on how he did it. He told me he wasn't sure. But sometime in the night, something told him to touch my hand. When he did, some sort of energy spike happened between us though I stayed asleep. So we came to the conclusion that Forrest is some sort of recharger which allows me to heal so many more people. And we've been traveling together ever since."

The story was romantic and all, but so unlikely. He never gave me any strength beyond the courage to con people. Forrest always found a way to survive. What had he done here?

Heidi leaned close and I could feel her focus before I saw it. She pointed at my foot and my face flushed when I saw the temp shoes I still wore. But she didn't seem to be bothered at all. "Would you like me to heal you now?"

The suggestion caught me off guard. My foot ached as if it begged me to try. The scars on my stomach pulled as I sat up straight. "How did you know?"

She smiled. "When we touched, I saw like a glow where your scars and still tender skin needed attention.

Miraculous indeed. "I don't want to hurt you."

Her smile made me think that must be what it was like when a saint looked upon you in love. "You won't. I've gained much more control over the past few months."

"But I'm not really sick anymore. You can save it for someone in dire need."

"If you were fully healed, the energy wouldn't have started to transfer at our accidental touch. Plus, I can't think of anyone I'd rather heal than Forrest's sister." She tapped her knee. "Put your foot here."

As my mind tried to think of more excuses to not use this generous soul, my leg lifted my foot. "I'm sorry I thought you were a fake."

"It's okay. Most people do. It's probably the only reason I don't get hauled off to an experimental lab or something." Heidi removed the temp shoe without even asking me why I was wearing them, then gripped her hands gently around the soles of my foot.

Instead of the sharp spike of energy I'd felt at our first touch, a gentle warming coursed through my skin. It flowed through me until it tickled my gut then my shoulder. Where she touched, however, the warmth turned hot. Pain flowed right underneath, but all healing involved pain. I could take it. The sensation was muted by my fascination as I felt and saw the glow ascend to my shoulder. As Heidi's energy seemed to re-focus on my stomach, Heidi's grip faltered. I yanked my foot away but managed to catch her before she fell off the small couch.

She was unresponsive. I saw her heal multiple people the other day. Why was she so weak this time? Dammit, I shouldn't have let her heal me. Maybe it was too much for one ability to interfere with another.

"Forrest!" I yelled.

The door flung open with my brother barreling through and Flores on his heels.

Forrest held Heidi up by her shoulders. "Heidi?" When she didn't respond, he turned to me and used the same accusatory tone I'd used on him "What did you do to her?"

"She insisted." I pleaded with Forrest who set Heidi back on the couch as she moaned and blinked her eyes open.

He seemed truly concerned, but how could I tell one way or another? He could be worried about Heidi or the money he was losing if she couldn't perform today. Yet, I'd called to him out of instinct when something went wrong. Even if he could be a selfish asshole, he wasn't a murderer. No way could the man who protected me all those years be that cold.

Flores asked, "What happened?"

In answer, I pulled aside the collar of my shirt to show him the once-mangled skin all pink and unblemished. His widened eyes mirrored the tightening of my throat at his surprise. The typically controlled emotional state of Flores was all over the place lately. I reached into Forrest's fridge and grabbed a beer. I had it opened and half downed before Heidi showed signs of movement. The lack of any pull from a scar in my shoulder hit me after I'd swallowed. To test the process, I bounced on the floor and was happily surprised that no hint of pain radiated from my foot.

With a tilt of the bottle to Heidi, I confessed to Flores. "She's the real deal."

Flores looked out the door, and I knew he was thinking about Austin. The fear that cramped my muscles wasn't my own. "I need to apologize."

"He loves you. He'll forgive you." I gulped the rest of the beer. I had to release Flores to deal with his relationship. "I have to get to the GRB and can walk from here. Why don't you take Austin home before the dreaded paperwork?"

The hard cop exterior faltered for a mere moment as he squeezed my hand. The warmth that radiated through me at his love for Austin was so similar to Heidi's gift, I wondered if love was what fueled the whole thing. The sentimental bullshit of that thought made me grab another beer from the fridge.

Chapter Twenty

When Flores left, I watched Forrest revive Heidi bit by bit. I guess he *could* give her energy back somehow, though I didn't feel a bit of it in the air like I had when she healed members of the audience. It could simply be a side effect of not being able to use my ability on Forrest at all.

After Heidi was able to sit up straight on her own, Forrest turned his attention on me. "Why did you bring that cop to my door?"

No reason to sugar coat it. "Because I saw an impression of you vomiting by a dumpster where a dead body was found." Maybe I should have made Flores stay for a minute. I was no good at interrogations, especially with my much quicker on his feet brother.

When he froze midway from lifting Heidi to a sitting position, I downed the rest of the second beer. If he confessed right now, I wouldn't even know where to go or what to do.

He recovered quickly though and smiled at Heidi's blinking eyes, even though his voice was laced with annoyance at my continued presence. "Well, it's quite a shock to the system when you're on a walk and see a dead body. Why don't you just go? And send Michelle in, would ya?"

"Fine." I slammed the bottle a bit too harshly on the laminate counter. Stomping my feet gave me so much satisfaction now that no pain accompanied the movement. I could get used to this. Though my bare foot reminded me I needed more substantial shoes. "Um, I couldn't borrow a pair of shoes, could I?"

Forrest scoffed as he brushed by me to start an electric kettle. "You and Heidi are the same size."

His ability to remember everything about everyone enraged me for no good reason. "How in the hell do you remember shit like that? And how do I know which shoes are Heidi's?"

Heidi spoke which brought me a bit of relief I didn't know I needed. "Check the bin under the bed."

My conscience couldn't handle having hurt her when she healed me after I thought she was a fake. I mean, I of all people should give others the benefit of the doubt when it came to odd abilities. I scowled at Forrest. He did this to me. He made me use my empathy to con unsuspecting people for money and it formed a permanent connection in my mind that people were always trying to con you.

Forrest ignored my glare and yelled out the door, "Michelle, I need you in here."

Michelle pushed through the door like she'd been waiting there for permission the whole time we argued.

I wanted all the answers. And I wanted them now. As I rummaged under the bed, I questioned Forrest. "Why didn't you call the police? What is your involvement in this whole nasty affair?"

My anger was overwhelmed with Michelle's, and I had to stop what I was doing to grab my gut as it severely cramped. Michelle pushed me back from the bed. "What are you doing, Fauna?"

As the pain shifted up making it difficult to breathe, I realized it wasn't anger I felt from Michelle. It was fear. I pointed to my bare feet since I couldn't seem to form words.

Michelle rolled her eyes and calmed down which released the squeeze on me. "Can you still not take care of yourself? It's pathetic."

"That's enough." Forrest defended me like he always had against her. *I guess some things never change.*

Heidi rubbed her forehead and looked between us. "What did I miss?"

Forrest's face tightened as if he realized he couldn't just avoid the subject. "My sister thinks I murdered someone last night. That's why she brought the cop here."

Michelle dropped a pair of black flats in my hands and pushed the bin under the bed. Eager to not cramp again, my body moved away from her while my mind reeled over what her reaction could possibly mean.

Heidi giggled, the sound so contradictory to the mood in the small space. "Don't be ridiculous, Fauna. Forrest couldn't hurt a fly. He's even a vegetarian now."

Was that a blush rising on my brother's cheeks?

"Plus, if you mean last night, he was with me here the whole time. He had to have been because I was at full power this morning. The only way that's ever happened was when he sleeps with me and uses whatever ability he has to recharge me."

Interesting, because I saw her in the vision too. They weren't here all night. Was she lying to protect him, or did she have no idea what he was up to? Heidi had been unconscious in the memory. When I tried to gauge Forrest's response, he turned away and brought a steaming cup of tea to Heidi. Even Michelle, who usually chose to glare at me, didn't meet my gaze as she exited the RV.

"Fauna will believe what she wants to believe." He seemed sad, not angry or defensive, but sad. "Now put the shoes on and go. We have people to help."

Apparently in no danger, Heidi sipped her tea.

When I opened the screen door without a single pull from my shoulder, I felt an immediate debt to Heidi. She might not think she was in danger, but I knew my brother. And Michelle was definitely hiding something.

Instinctively, I held open the door as Michelle lead in a young Hispanic man who played his fingers on his pants like the keys of a piano. "Right this way, Mr. Hernandez," Michelle said.

His round cheeks and bouncy walk showed no outward sign of illness. Beyond a bath, the man didn't seem to need anything at all. Besides, after Heidi fainted with my healing, surely she didn't have the energy to heal another right now. Not if her power worked the way she said it did. He hummed "I Could Fall in Love" by Selena in such perfect pitch, I'd have bet he had a gorgeous voice. As the screen door closed, I swore I saw Heidi leaned back against the couch blinking at Mr. Hernandez with a weak smile, then she closed her eyes. It looked like she had fallen asleep.

Michelle slammed the inside door before I could make any further observations. After a deep breath to contain the scream I wanted to release, I considered what to do next. The urge to help someone was overwhelming. My ability seemed like a parlor trick compared to Heidi's.

My phone buzzed with a text from Amelia asking if I was done yet.

That was my in, my opportunity to give back. St. Benedict's needed new computers and the GRB across the street was full of companies with deep pockets. Time to do some good for once. I'd solve the Forrest problem later. There wasn't much I could do without Detective Flores anyway. For the first time in a long time, I headed out for a walk without any fear of the distance. My foot could take it. That high alone might get me through the day.

Chapter Twenty-One

Once again, I found myself on the outskirts of the growing crowd centered around the healer. But this time, I'd brought the big guns. After I'd secured multiple offers of new computers and hardware to fix the Wi-Fi at St. Benedict's, Amelia wanted to head home. We had stayed out late Tuesday and I didn't blame her, but I wasn't done for the night. I still had questions I needed answered and only one group could help me.

So I called the Collected. I'd never requested help, but I pulled out a big ask for this one. All of them couldn't make it on a Wednesday night, but I didn't want to wait until Friday. Forrest might have packed up and gone before then. I had to move fast.

Belinda squeezed my elbow and shook her head. She didn't sense any empaths nearby. To be honest, I didn't know if she could even sense a healer. Heidi's ability was so different than ours. Yet, each of our abilities were different varieties. I'd never forget when Debra explained it to me that first night I met the Collected. I'd never missed her more than tonight. She would have known exactly what to do to welcome Heidi into our ranks.

Ademi wore a bright orange scarf on her head today. She'd become our de facto leader, and we all looked to her when we attempted to go anywhere as a group. "How's everyone doing? This will be just as bad as the Nutcracker Market. If anyone wants to leave, now's the time."

So many places with a bunch of people swirled with differing emotions until the muddy mess gave me such a headache I had to leave. Even the dance clubs I totally enjoyed had a mix which was why I used alcohol to tame the insecurities and depression and just emphasize the intense lust. That was where the high came from. Heidi's fans had some other emotions floating just below the surface, such as confusion and fear, but mostly it was hope. What a wonderful feeling. While lust tickled all my sexual centers and made my skin sing with sensation, hope made my fingers and toes tingle and my chest swell like it had just discovered oxygen for the first time. I hadn't experienced it in such quantities since my time when I traveled with Forrest regularly. I supposed that was one thing he was good at building in people: hope. But was that a service to the community if it was false, if you ripped it away as soon as their payment cleared?

Enrique seemed to be enjoying the high as much as I was. "I'm not going anywhere. Let's see this show."

Rodney's deep voice didn't carry as far as I was used to with so many bodies so close by. "So we're here to read you brother?"

"More his current companion, Heidi. She's a healer, and I want to make sure she knows she's not alone." I tilted my head back and forth, trying to make up my mind. "Though if any of you can get anything out of Forrest, I'd be impressed. My powers don't work on him and neither do Heidi's."

Belinda squeezed me and her support warmed my core. She still hadn't talked. None of us knew whether it was a psychological condition or a physiological one, but we also didn't care. She was perfect the way she was.

"If anyone gets anything, we'll let you know." Ademi looked each one of us in the face, as if she were trying to get her children to obey. "And if anyone needs help or needs out, tell us immediately. We're here to help, not hurt or get injured."

THE HEALER

Surely, Forrest couldn't resist all of our powers. At least one of us should be able to get through. What if we did find out that Heidi needed to get away or that Forrest really was a murderer? He'd know we knew probably before we did. He was good like that. I should have called Flores for backup. Forrest wouldn't get very far with HPD keeping an eye on him.

Why hadn't I called Flores to make sure he was all right? It hadn't even occurred to me. I was the worst friend ever and deserved to be alone.

Before my train of thought killed my high, the audience roared with cheering and whistles and joy on top of the hope. The vast majority of these people didn't need a healer, they wanted to witness a miracle. While stretching to my tip toes to see over the person in front of me, not a single twinge of pain cramped my foot. I'd been a part of a miracle already this morning, and I was still eager to witness another. If what Heidi could do wasn't a miracle, then there was no such thing. I hoped her healing of me didn't leave her too weak to help someone in true need.

Forrest practically pounced on the stage. Someone had bolstered the base and it looked much stronger than before.

Enrique cracked his knuckles. "If that's him, I bet I could get something out of him."

My nipples tingled with Enrique's lust. Through his eyes, I could see why he was so attracted. My brother did make a pretty picture. I guess I didn't always notice because his inside was so rotten.

Rodney elbowed Enrique. "Stop it," he complained as he adjusted his pants. "Some of us are trying to concentrate."

With a wink, Enrique flared the lust making all of us squirm, then shut it off. "Sorry. Sometimes, I can't help it."

Maybe bringing them here was a mistake. If Forrest discovered what they could do, he very well might con one or more of the Collected to travel with him.

Surprisingly, Heidi climbed up right behind Forrest without

any assistance. Her rosy cheeks and easy stride slackened my guilt. Apparently, Forrest's special ability had recharged her somehow, exactly like she claimed. A man who could do that wouldn't kill to protect his secret, would he? He wanted people to know about Heidi. Judging by the crowd, it wouldn't be long before these two filled stadiums like he always wanted to do with me. As I very well might have agreed to if not for Sylvia. And I was a fake. I couldn't speak to the dead. Heidi was the real thing.

Ademi interrupted my internal monologue. "We need to get closer if we're going to be of any use."

While we obeyed and moved forward, I studied Heidi. She looked happy, if not comfortable, under full scrutiny. Forrest certainly hadn't forced her to take the stage. After spending just a few minutes with her, I knew she wanted to help people. Something was itching the back of my mind though, something I was missing.

Belinda gasped when we were just a few feet into the crowd. She held up three fingers and motioned toward the stage.

I asked, "Three of them?" How could she sense anything over the cheering and hope-filled crowd we were now surrounded by? Let alone three gifted?

Plus, there were only two on the stage. The others in the Collected seemed as confused as I was.

Enrique moved in a circle around us making the people on our perimeter nervous enough to give us some space.

After tilting her head in approval, Ademi asked Belinda. "Are you sure?"

Belinda's emphatic nod communicated she was positive.

Forrest continued his hype speech, much the same as it had been a couple days before, but he seemed to only be speaking to us. I spotted Michelle's blue hair for a second, but then she blended into the crowd, and I lost her. Heidi was the only other person on the stage, and she interacted with the crowd eagerly reaching out to touch her. She managed to stay just out of range. I couldn't imagine the nightmare that would ensue if she lost her balance and fell in among them. Those sensible shoes she wore would prevent any slippage. I never dressed so conservatively when I'd take the stage. Heels and shiny jewelry was my MO. If an adoring crowd was going to ogle me, I had to feel confident, didn't I?

Her shoes. Her sensible, flat, peach-colored shoes. Holy shit. The shoes she wore were identical to the single one Henrietta showed me at St. Benedict's, the one she said came from the Shadows. Michelle had had a fit when I tried to get shoes for myself. Was Heidi involved in all of this and Forrest was really the innocent one? She told me an entire tragic back story, and I totally fell for it.

The crowd silenced. Not for anyone else. They still cheered and chanted "Healer" and clapped and stomped. But any emotion I'd felt from them sunk to the back of my senses, replaced by an intense, personal sense of dread. Forrest *was* involved. There were too many coincidences for me to ignore, and he'd never be the innocent one.

I walked away from my friends and headed toward the RV. I must have missed something. How did I not feel that same sort of signature imprint in the RV but I did at each location of the mysterious deaths. At this point, I was with Collins; they weren't suicides. Someone took these people's lives, all to protect Forrest's interests. If only I could sense my brother's true feelings, maybe I would have known all the way back then that he was capable of such evil. I knew he could twist the murders, hide them, and get away with it. He was certainly smart enough. I never imagined he was cold-hearted enough.

Of course the door was locked. No one seemed to be guarding it though. Around the back, I could just reach the window Austin tried to crawl out of earlier. Had that just been today? I wasn't sure how I would get up there. But if the shoes were here, then the serrated knife had to be too. There was no way the instrument used to take these lives wouldn't have an impression left on it. I could identify it and bring Flores here with a search warrant before my brother could skip town and pull the same shit in another city.

On the side of the RV laid a pile of broken bits and pieces I guessed they'd cleared from the parking lot or maybe someone just dumped it all there. Though everything in that area seemed shrouded in darkness, I thought I felt something, that signature but weak. I brushed it off. It was dark outside and the makeshift lights they had facing the stage made everything else feel like it was in the shadows and I was being paranoid.

As I pulled a half-broken chair under the window, Michelle popped up right next to me. The shock of her sudden appearance made me drop the chair right on my foot. The pain rocked through my joint. When I pulled it up to hold the fresh injury, the combination of uneven pavement and unbalanced mind caused me to fall flat on my butt with a jarring bite of my lower lip.

I rubbed the blood from my lip and attempted to stand. The pain in my foot made me want to laugh and cry at the same time. "Come on, Michelle. You scared the shit out of me. You could have said something."

Even in the dark, her smirk was unmistakable. "I should have announced myself before stopping a thief from breaking into our home?"

She put a hand on my shoulder and my gut clenched with her fury. What was she so mad about? I knew she didn't like me, but this was something wholly different. As I analyzed the feeling, all other emotions faded, with the fury leaving last. I thought this was what other people feel like, just their own emotions with everyone else a blank slate. Until I realized all of *my* emotions were also gone. I could call them by name: fear, surprise, anger, but none of them affected me. Actually, I felt so calm and relaxed I sat back against the RV.

I blinked up at Michelle who was backlit like an angel. Her hand comforted me. Somehow, I knew she'd watch over me while I napped. It had been a rough week. I could use a bit of shut eye. A shot of adrenaline made me jump like when you're falling asleep and your body believes you're falling. Rapid blinking cleared my unfocused gaze long enough to see a flash in Michelle's eye.

Her voice soothed the spike of emotion that coursed through me until I couldn't even remember why I was scared. "Shhh, I've got you."

"Michelle?" My voice didn't sound like me. It was low and whispery and mechanical, like my own voice was only an imitation. Shouldn't I be terrified? The thought was no more than a warning in tiny letters on a candy bar and I paid it just as much attention.

"I've got you, Fauna." Michelle sounded like my mom on one of her good days. It was what love sounded like.

I smiled up at her. "You've got me."

She continued to tell me to lay down and rest. It would all be over soon. And the only thing I wanted to do was please her. Everything in my body quieted; it was the most peaceful feeling I'd ever experienced. Light glimmered from something in Michelle's hand and a flash of Phil Tanner breached the quiet of my mind. He couldn't be back. Heidi had just healed me. I wanted to wear heels again. What was I thinking about?

Something wasn't right and I knew I had to get out of there. My heart pumped and I tried to sit up, but I felt drugged.

Michelle touched my forehead with the tips of her fingers. "Why are you always so difficult? Just lay down and go to sleep."

All of my flippant concerns fled, and everything inside calmed down again. I didn't have anything to worry about.

"Fauna?" Ademi's voice floated in the air from far away.

My shoulders were pulled up and my head rested on the shoulder of a man who smelled exactly like Rodney. Fear in his voice didn't react with my body at all. So odd. "She's, well, she's empty, like a shell of Fauna with her essence quieted to the point of unrecognition."

"Can you wake it up?"

A shadow fell across my face. At least I thought it was a shadow. My eyes were closed. I couldn't remember how to open them. My mouth worked though. "Michelle was helping me sleep."

A stomping foot on the ground tickled my ears and opened my eyes. Huh, that wasn't so hard. How did I forget how to do that? A tiny, but fiery, woman with cropped hair that flew around her head as she gesticulated, pointed to the side of the trailer.

Ademi's rhythmic voice woke me further. "I understand, Belinda. But I didn't see a thing. Did anyone else?"

Rodney replied, "Nothing but shadow. It's pretty dark back here."

As my awareness reawakened, my eye twitched slightly with his worry. With a gentle push, I pulled myself up off the ground. A pain in my foot had me momentarily panicked until I remembered that I'd dropped the chair on it when Michelle scared me. The old injury hadn't returned.

Where was Michelle anyway? "Did anyone see a girl with blue hair nearby?"

Belinda stomped her foot again and pointed to the side of the trailer.

Rodney helped me to my feet as Enrique and Ademi searched the shadows.

Ademi shook her head. "There's no one back here."

Enrique feathered his thick, dark hair back with nervous fingers. He was also trying to go gloveless like me, with the same mixed results. If Debra could do it, we could too, right? "Belinda confirmed Heidi is definitely one of us, though her colors are a little different. Your brother is the big question mark."

Huh, I assumed Forrest was some flavor of empath since he could recharge Heidi. "You know, my powers don't work on Forrest. I've never been able to sense what he's feeling."

Ademi nodded at Belinda's quick hand movements. "She says his aura is missing. She's never see anything like it. Even non-empaths have an aura, but not your brother."

The entire concept was so new, I didn't know what to do with that information. Plus, I felt like I was forgetting something else.

As we walked around the trailer back to the chanting crowd, Heidi's power vibrated from the stage as she held onto a frail young man.

"Healer! Healer!" rang through the parking lot.

It really did help the concentration because every other emotion disappeared as the audience focused on their chant and the stage. A glance at my fellow empaths told me they felt the same. So near to the stage, I could see the look of ecstasy on the ill man's pale face. I remembered the feeling well. As color returned to his cheeks and his body loosened from extinguished pain, I felt something else. I closed my eyes to explore what that odd sensation was.

While Heidi did her thing, I could trace the healing power. It was like a part of me was pulled to the man's bones where I could feel the imbalance. I rode with Heidi as she mended the cells within, the ones not functioning properly. Somehow, they seemed highlighted like when I got a copy of last year's test in college. All the right answers were circled, and I just had to make the corrections in the body itself.

What was happening? Whatever disconnect I'd felt after falling from the chair behind the trailer dissipated, and I stumbled away from the chanting and the healing. Forrest's eyes focused on me, his head cocked like a curious dog. I just shook mine.

Not as affected as the rest of the group, Rodney stayed by my side as I moved to the back of the crowd. "Are you okay?"

I could barely hear him above the chanting, and I couldn't feel anything. The remnant of the man's illness, of Heidi's power, haunted me. It was like when I just knew I could reflect my pain onto Phil Tanner. A moment of clarity was all it took for me to do what Albert Johnson could do. Did I pick up Heidi's ability? Could I heal?

Fuck. The last thing I needed was more responsibility.

I turned to Rodney and swished a tear from my eye. "Could I trouble you for a ride home?"

He immediately pulled his keys from his pocket. "It's no trouble."

Chapter Twenty-Two

My phone woke me up the next morning. Well, more like it disturbed my drunken stupor. I'd drained most of what I had in the house after Rodney dropped me off. I couldn't face whatever it was that I experienced last night. It had to have been because I bumped my head when I fell off that chair. Why had I been trying to crawl in the window anyway. Everything was so blurry.

I drug myself out of bed to drink right out of my bathroom faucet. I did this often enough, you'd think I'd keep a glass here or something. The strong sunlight through the blinds told me it wasn't early, but I wasn't ready to face the harsh daylight. Was I supposed to open the store today? Obviously, Amelia wasn't picking me up for anything or I would have been awoken by her honking outside. What day was it?

As I picked up my phone to check, it rang again, and I almost dropped it in the sink.

It was Flores and my heart stopped. He would've texted if it wasn't important. "There's another body."

His voice had a bit of a waver in it. "No. I was calling to see if you'd be up to questioning the prisoner. I got an emergency pass for this afternoon."

Emergency pass couldn't be good. The fact that he still called him "the prisoner" couldn't be good either.

"Of course, I can." My growling stomach demanded attention first. "Meet at Dish Society?"

He hesitated, but acquiesced. "Sure."

As I unabashedly shoved a huge forkful of poached egg, homemade cream gravy, buttermilk biscuit, and fried chicken into my drooling mouth, Flores quietly sipped his black coffee and stared at his avocado toast. Time to get him to talk. "Okay, fess up. What's really going on?"

Flores took a slow sip of his coffee then set down the mug. He looked up at me and the back of my jaw ached from his sadness. "Remember my abuela and how I'm pretty sure she was like you, could do the things you can do."

He seemed to be struggling so I filled in the blank. "She was an empath."

Flores nodded once, staring into his coffee like it would guide him through his painful story. "That loving woman touched each of us on the cheek every time we came to visit her. Though Mom swore up and down that Abuela could read people's minds, I never believed she had any sort of magical ability—"

"It's not magical." For some reason, that description offended me. I didn't know why. Because magic wasn't real and I was, maybe?

Flores looked up at me with his head still down in that sexy way that made me lose my train of thought. "Well, I don't know what else to call it." He took in a deep breath and dived into the story like I'd not interrupted. "Anyway, she'd touch each of us on the cheek every Sunday when we'd come by after church, and she'd always say something that was insightful. As I got older, I figured out that Mom told her whatever we were having trouble with that week and Abuela would give us comfort or reprimand us if we were wrong."

His words fell off and he stared into space. I swallowed the last bite of biscuit and spurred him forward. "Were there a lot of you? Like did you have a big family?"

Flores shrugged. "Normal size I'd say. There were a lot of cousins running around. We grew up more like siblings, if I use Austin's way of describing family relationships. And we weren't always on the right side of the law. Poor kids with nothing to do causing trouble, it's almost too mundane to describe. When I became a teenager, Pedro, my cousin who was the same age as me, and I did everything together. We could have been twins, not just in appearance, but in the way we saw the world. It didn't care about us, so we didn't care about it. We were inseparable and of the same mind and refused to follow any rules. We were too cool for school. We'd ditch and commit misdemeanors all over town."

I couldn't help it. I laughed. "Commit misdemeanors? I'm sure that's what you said you were doing. Can't turn the cop off, can you?"

The hint of a smile that washed across his face did nothing to lighten the sadness I felt from him. "Why would I want to turn it off? It saved me." He cracked his neck and sat back. "Abuela called us out one Sunday."

For some reason, the routine of grandma's house and the hooligan teenagers didn't mash up for me. "You still went to Abuela's?"

This time, the smile was genuine, and the tips of my fingers tingled. "We would never miss out on homemade tortillas and Abuela's rojo enchilada salsa. No one makes the red sauce like Abuela." He rubbed his eye, then kept going. "So she touched us both on the cheek, then yelled at us for half an hour with the entire family looking on. You see, that week we'd beaten up a younger boy because he'd told the corner store owner that we'd stolen from his store. I don't know how she knew. You can't read minds, right?"

A shake of my head answered his question. "My guess? You were feeling guilty, and you spilled the details while she reprimanded you."

Flores stared at the ceiling, seemingly reliving the memory. I wondered if that was what I looked like when I fell into a memory. "Damn, you're right. I definitely was feeling guilty and with her interrogating me, my sweet, kind grandma, I spilled. That explains why Pedro was so mad at me. Because after that day, my mom kept a tighter leash and Pedro refused to let me go with him. Somewhere in that timeframe, I decided to change sides and help stop punks like me instead of running around with them."

This part I could guess. "So you became a cop."

"I did." He took a long sip of coffee. "Only a couple years out of the academy, Pedro's criminal career had really taken off. The first murder scene I'd ever walked into had Pedro's fingerprints all over it. The kid was a drug dealer who was encroaching on Pedro's territory. I knew what had happened. Pedro had been escalating in violence for years now. No matter how many times I warned him, no matter how many fights we got into at Abuela's, he wouldn't listen. I had to do my duty. I was the arresting officer and took him in.

"Abuela came to court every day during his trial. In the middle of it, she got close enough to touch Pedro's cheek, like she'd done hundreds of times. She kissed him on the forehead before the bailiff made her take a seat. I helped her and she took my head in her hands to stare directly into my eyes. 'He's innocent, mijo. You have to help him.' That's all she said. Of course, I didn't believe her. I'd seen the evidence and it wasn't just circumstantial. There was hard scientific proof tying Pedro to the murder. With no alibi, he had no way to dispute it."

The deep sadness returned. "Pedro was sentenced to life in prison with no chance of parole. On Abuela's death bed, the very last words she said to me were 'Help your cousin. Pedro is innocent.' I took it as the last words of a desperate grandmother who thought nothing but good things about her grandchildren." His hand weakly gestured to me.

I guessed where he was going. "And then you met me and reconsidered what your abuela could do."

He nodded. "What if she had been telling the truth the whole time? What if Pedro was innocent of this murder and I'd helped put my first best friend, my closest cousin, into prison for life? And now he's terminally ill and I can't stand the thought of him withering away in prison instead of taking his last breath around family."

More pieces of the puzzle fell into place. "That's why Austin searched for the healer. It was Pedro he was trying to save."

My heart beat a bit faster with the love Flores felt for his husband. I could have that someday, right? "Austin means well. He sees me deal with people's pain all day and he wanted to help me with mine."

Time to lighten the mood. "Well, eat up. We've got a drive ahead of us. Let's go see what your abuela saw in your cousin."

"Fauna?"

"Yes?"

"Thank you."

Chapter Twenty-Three

Flores was completely silent and calm on our way to the prison. Considering he'd just talked more than I'd heard him talk ever, even at a party, I'm sure he'd made his word quota for the day. His return to his taciturn nature allowed me the time to center myself and put up my barriers before entering the prison. Good thing too. I was nowhere near the general population. Still, the walls vibrated with the range of emotions embedded within. This would have been a house of horrors if I'd not learned anything about how to protect myself.

I pushed my nervousness to the front of my mind and allowed my mom's hymn to act as a barrier to anything else. Who knew that embracing my emotions would aid me at suppressing the intrusion of others. It worked though. When a stern white man in denial about his impending baldness shook my hand, I didn't feel a thing.

After the warden welcomed us, he got right down to business. There must be a class at the academy that taught seriousness. "Detective, he insisted on sitting up in a normal visiting room. He should be lying down and it's nothing beyond sheer stubbornness that's keeping him upright."

Flores nodded. "I would expect nothing less. We'll be quick."

The warden nodded permission to the uniformed guard at the door of what looked very much like the interrogation room at 1200 Travis. Inside the room on the other side of the table sat Pedro. His skin had no color, and he stared at us with sunken eyes that still managed to convey anger. The chair was pushed very close to the table where his hands were cuffed. He was so skinny the cuffs likely didn't need to be attached to the table at all. I'd have been surprised to see him lift his arms under their weight. A folded wheelchair leaned against the far wall. The guards must have respected Pedro. Otherwise, why would they have protected his dignity by transferring him to the flat-backed chair.

When Flores pulled out a chair for me, I realized I'd been taking in the scene too long. He looked almost as pale as his cousin. This was painful for both of them.

Pedro spoke first, taking control of the conversation. Despite his failing health, his voice rang out deep and strong. "Why did you request this meeting, Mateo? Come to see your criminal cousin breathe his last?"

Flores puffed up and his cheeks flushed. "Why did *you* agree to this meeting?"

Pedro dropped his head but looked up with his eyes in the exact same way Flores usually did. This was going to be creepier than I thought. I needed to separate the two in my mind before I took a reading. I couldn't let my favorable thoughts of Flores influence the blank slate I needed to judge Pedro's reactions. "I wanted you to see what you did to family."

"Me? I didn't—"

I interrupted before they screamed at each other until Pedro was too worn out to answer any questions. "Do you know what your abuela could do?"

Both men froze, just staring at each other. Pedro answered, "I do. Mateo never believed. He was foolish in that way."

I shook my head at Flores without turning around. I'd seen more of his human side and less of his detective side this week.

He sure did have a temper. "Pedro, I'm Fauna. And I can do what your abuela could. Flor ... Mateo has seen proof and he believes. Will you let me do a reading?"

The prisoner seemed to deflate a bit. My barriers were tight, and I couldn't tell what he was feeling: relief or resignation. "What good would it do? I didn't kill the kid, but I'm dying anyway."

Resignation then. "We might be able to find the real killer and clear your name."

Flores sat down in the chair next to me. "And your son will know the truth about his father."

Pedro leaned down and flicked a tear from his eye with a bound hand. There was something so fragile in the movement. "You can touch me."

As I moved my hand forward ready to let Pedro and only Pedro through my wall, the guard by the door took a step forward. Flores waved him off without looking up. He concentrated on my hand, as if a buzzer would go off to tell him whether Pedro was innocent or guilty.

It was quite pleasant touching someone who wasn't out of control, especially when my mind was clear and ready for the encounter. Pedro's emotions swirled with fear and regret that clenched my gut and hollowed my chest. Everything was on the surface for him. He wasn't nearly as guarded as Flores. So they did possess some differences.

A slight smile creased Pedro's wan face. "You feel like her, warm. Can you speak with her?"

Flashes of past transgressions filled my mind. I couldn't go back to that. "No, but I can experience what you're feeling which is probably what she could do."

Flores chuckled. "Remember when we stole those bikes from those kids?"

Pedro laughed in almost the same manner. "She wouldn't let it go at Sunday dinner until she dragged it out of us. And then she marched us to the bikes and made us return them."

"After we washed them and oiled the chains." Flores real laughter bounced in the hard room.

My stomach unclenched as my fingers and toes tickled. Pedro was easy to read. He wasn't hiding anything. Yet.

With a nod, Flores said, "And that's exactly the point. We thought Abuela could read our minds, but she couldn't, just what we were feeling. She'd know we were feeling smug and a bit elusive which means we'd done wrong. So she'd badger us until we confessed and it made her look all knowing."

All of Pedro's emotions calmed again, quieting any reaction of my body. "Which is why you're here. Abuela told you I didn't murder anyone. You found her"—he gestured to me and the back of my eye throbbed, but just for one beat—"and now you believe your family."

"Come on, Pedro. You know the evidence pointed to you and you know your silence didn't help your case."

Pedro pulled back but my hand went with him for the mere inches he could move. As his anger flared, I felt something else. Not a reaction in my body, but a reaction in his. Something in his chest vibrated. It wasn't his heart. I could feel his pulse which was fast at the moment, but perfectly rhythmic. What was that odd element?

As he always managed to do, Flores took a deep breath and calmed his temper. "Just tell us what happened that night."

Pedro managed the same with his temper, but I still felt that odd thing in his chest. I had no idea what emotion that evoked. Oh God, please don't let me mess this up for Flores. I opened myself wider to make sure I didn't make any mistakes. The residual anger from Flores and concern from the guard at the door floated over Pedro's emotions. I could handle that much, and it would help me stay focused on what I searched for: the truth.

After taking my fingers into his hand like he needed the comfort of a friend, Pedro told his story. Through what he was doing that day—minor crime attached to minor guilt—to when he found the body, Pedro spilled it all. Not once did I feel a lie: no rise in heart rate, no guilt at the scene of the murder, just a little horror at what had happened, no fear of discovery. He laid it all out and I was 100 percent convinced of his innocence. For the murder anyway. This particular man looked at the world in a more complex way than I ever had, judging by the range of emotions he felt describing that day. Black and white never occurred to him. Everything was gray.

Once he was done, I squeezed his hand gently and released him. "He didn't do it, Flores. I can't tell you who did, but I can tell you that this man sitting here did not kill that boy."

Flores leaned back against his chair. "Then I guess I better get to work."

Pedro looked through the ceiling and lifted his hands as far as the cuffs attached to the table would let him. "Gracias, Abuela."

Then he bent almost in half with a violent coughing attack. Since I'd lowered my barriers, his pain bounced in my chest. For a moment, I couldn't breathe and hated the torment the sick man must be going through. Wishing I could help him, I looked up as Flores moved to the other side of the table and motioned to the guard to release Pedro from the table. Through the white cotton of his prison garb, I swore I saw specks of light, like bioluminescence behind boats in the middle of the night. What was that?

The men were so distracted, they didn't notice me join them until I flattened my hand on Pedro's chest.

"Fauna, you have to stay on the other side of the table." Flores's voice tried to persuade me to move, but I had to know what was happening.

I ignored everyone else and focused on Pedro. "Do you have lung cancer?" I made an educated guess.

Through his ragged breathing, Pedro nodded. "Terminal."

I didn't know how I knew, but I could kill those cells. I could see them and feel them.

Flores's hand closed over my free hand. "Fauna, what are you doing?"

I blinked up at him as the guard started to pull Pedro to his wheelchair. "I don't know how, but I can help him. I know how Heidi does it."

"Wait," he said to the guard. Hope, just like at the gathered crowd, burst over the fear and worry Flores had been feeling. "Are you sure?"

With a reassuring smile, I turned to Pedro and put one hand on his chest and one on his forehead. "Close your eyes and think happy thoughts."

Pedro's cough had subsided, but his pain had not. It hit me like a freight train. How could anyone handle this much agony and still be upright? As if my body agreed with me, I fell to one knee.

Flores's fear overwhelmed the pain when he grabbed my elbow. "No."

Why was everyone trying to save me from the effects of my empathy? If this was a gift, not a curse, as had been hammered into my mind for months now, then I would use it in any way I saw fit. It was time for me to be in control.

My anger thwarted his and I yanked my elbow back. "I don't need your protection. I can do this."

He blinked at me, but acquiesced with his hands in his pocket, as if he didn't trust himself to obey my wishes. The guard just looked confused. He must have heard everything we'd said, but none of it made sense from an outside point of view. But he also had some sort of loyalty to Pedro, that much was obvious. After receiving a nod from the dying man, the guard stepped back.

Quickly, before Flores changed his mind, I put both hands on Pedro's chest. Expecting the pain this time, it didn't drop me. With my eyes closed, I could feel where each pocket of misbehaving cells grew and multiplied. I could stop them. Was this what Heidi did? Something from deep inside me poured into

Pedro, like my immune system aiding his with energy that attacked the cells and killed them, one after another. The world outside faded in layers as more energy attacked the cancer cells. I couldn't see every cell or even his organs like on the Magic School Bus. Instead, it was more like sensing emotions. That glow I saw wasn't a physical manifestation, it was a psychic one. One kind of energy against another and the cancer didn't have a chance.

The pain faded and Pedro's chest expanded without a twinge of difficulty. Almost there. I wasn't a doctor but I knew you couldn't leave any cells behind. My mind, that usually searched for emotional clues and judged their validity with my physical reactions, sought and destroyed any hint of glow which included a few clusters outside of the chest area. Everything else turned dark: the room, Flores's voice, Pedro's movement.

I opened my eyes to pitch black. "Who turned out the lights?" I asked.

As I tried to stand on what felt like dead tree trunks instead of legs, I realized I couldn't maintain my balance and tumbled backward. Weak. I felt so exhausted. I just needed to sleep. A little nap would do me ...

Chapter Twenty-Four

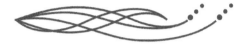

Fluorescent lights hurt my eyes as I blinked them open. I tried to lift my hand to protect them, but my arm was so heavy and tangled in some sort of cord. Panic gripped me as I remembered last time I was tied to a bed. My body shot up, fueled by adrenaline, fully alert. A thin blanket fell off of me, and my arms were weighted down by so many lines.

Tucker's warm hands closed over my shoulders and the dimple in his left cheek practically shown with the huge smile plastered on his face. Were those tears on his cheeks? "Well, that's a good sign. A spark of that kind of energy has to mean you're feeling better."

Before I yanked out the lines in my arms, I realized they were IVs and I was in the hospital. But I couldn't remember how I'd gotten there. "What happened?" Sudden exhaustion hit me, like I hadn't slept in days. The weakness sapped my momentary burst of energy, and I sagged against Tucker.

While situating me against the fluff-less pillow and checking the IVs, Tucker told me what he knew. "Flores said you'd been helping him question a witness and you passed out. The prison hospital reported the symptoms, which sounded remarkably like the Wasting, so I had you transferred down here. I'm sorry,

Fauna. You must have been exposed at St. Benedict's. Did you eat or drink anything while you were there?"

Nurses of multiple shapes and ages and genders flooded through the door of my room. Except it wasn't my room. Now that I had an idea of where I was and why, I took a look around. I was in a ward of some sort with multiple beds separated by curtains. It brought to mind that scene in Tombstone when Doc Holliday lay dying and Wyatt Earp came to say good-bye.

Fear flushed my cheeks. "Am I dying?"

Tucker let out a long breath. "Until you sat up just now, I'm not sure what the answer would be. It's the biggest bit of hope I've seen yet. I'm sorry, Fauna. I can't find the cause. We've traced it to Dallas, then Shreveport, then Little Rock, but we can't figure out how it's transmitted or any effective treatment. The CDC has been called to aide in the investigation. They've got a bigger database and more tools. Maybe they can make sense of this."

Another medical professional in white scrubs made her way between Tucker and I. "Ms. Young, I'm Dr. Fountain. You were asleep for quite a while. How do you feel?"

I'd slept awhile, huh? Tucker hadn't told me how long I'd been out. He grabbed his phone and typed away like whatever was happening wasn't any of his concern. Asshole!

Whew! That came out of nowhere. I apparently had zero control over my emotions right now. How would I be able to control input from others? I didn't like this at all. I wondered how I could convince them to let me go home and recover there.

With the new doctor's no-nonsense attitude, I doubted that would be an option. Still, I felt like an open wound without any of my protections up. I couldn't even remember what my mom's voice sounded like to start my mantra. When she touched my arm to check an IV, I flinched expecting a rush of emotions. Instead, I felt nothing.

Dr. Fountain studied my face. "Does that hurt?" She probed my skin from my fingertips to my shoulder.

"No." It didn't hurt. Nothing hurt. I just felt weak, like Pedro had been.

What happened came back all at once. I'd seen his cancer, like physically saw it. That had never happened to me before. A friend of mine in high school died of leukemia and I hadn't seen a thing. I'd felt the inconsolable grief of her family at the funeral but no sign of illness. I'd cured Pedro. I knew I had. Something deep down had taken over and I poured health into him, strengthening his immune system and targeting those cancer cells. It was like something out of a science fiction movie. Ridiculous. I couldn't heal people. Only Heidi could do that. What was happening?

My stomach growled in protest. Before I could answer any of these questions, I needed to eat. "Can I have a sandwich?"

I'd never seen a more Spock-like eyebrow in my life. Dr. Fountain could have been part Vulcan herself. "You're hungry? That's a great sign. Why don't we start with chicken broth and see where we go from there."

When she pushed my hair off my forehead, I felt a jolt of energy that brought warmth to my cold fingers and toes. Dr. Fountain grabbed the side rails of the bed with both hands. Tucker came forward to catch her if she fell. And I thought he was only my savior. Heroes would hero with everyone, I supposed.

She managed to smile weakly and wave him away. "I suppose I could use a bite to eat as well."

A handsome young nurse startled me when he spoke from the other side of the bed. It was weird to be surrounded by people but unable to sense them. "I'll put in the order for the broth. If you'll come with me, Dr. Fountain, I'll show you to the cafeteria. The breakfast is actually quite good."

She shook her head at him and moved to the nearby sink to wash her hands. "I'll be fine, Michael. It's just been a long day."

When my eyes burned reflecting Michael's disappointment, tears popped into them. I could sense him. My empathy wasn't gone, just temporarily silent. Who would have guessed a year ago that I'd be happy the gift hadn't burned out permanently? I'd just started to learn how to use it to help others without ruining my own life. I didn't want it to stop now.

An alarm beeped on another bed further back in the ward. Dr. Fountain dried her hands and motioned Nurse Michael toward the alarm.

"Dr. Wickman," it took me a minute to realize she meant Tucker, "I'll leave this patient in your care. Please inform me if there are any changes."

"Of course," he answered.

"CDC?" I asked.

"The first wave. Dr. Fountain's here to see if they need to call out the big guns or if I'm just a city doctor trying to make a name for himself." He took my hand in the most welcome bedside manner I could have envisioned. His warmth enveloped me better than any blanket until I realized it felt an awful lot like love.

With renewed strength, I yanked my hand away. To cover up my obvious rejection, I scratched my shoulder where the scar used to be.

Instead of being hurt, Tucker leaned forward and pulled back the gown slightly. "Wow! Your scar has faded to almost nothing. It's remarkable."

Oh shit. How was I going to explain that? Well, it was getting too real anyway. I supposed it was time to break it all off. After a deep breath, I pulled the cover from my foot displaying the smooth, unscarred skin. "Well, there are probably some things I should tell you."

He probed the area gently. "I don't even feel scarred tissue beneath the skin."

His touch sent shocks through me, and my entire body vibrated with warmth. Energy filled my soul and for a moment I wondered if I could fly. Then I noticed Tucker's eyelids drooping. Hurriedly, I pushed him off of me so we weren't touching and yelled for Dr. Fountain.

She must not have gotten too far down the hallway, because she rushed back through the doors to check on Tucker. His eyes blinked lazily, but he didn't fall down or pass out. What Heidi told me about her healing ability and how it bounced back by stealing energy from healthy people if she wasn't careful haunted me. Is that what had happened? Had I healed Pedro, weakened myself to coma level, then stolen Tucker's vitality to recover?

I had to have cut off connection before any permanent damage, right? I'd broken up with guys before to protect myself from their stares or accusations of insanity. But this time, I was going to have to end it to protect him. This man was way too good for me and certainly didn't deserve to be physically harmed because of me. Was I ever going to get my shit together?

It was all fucking ridiculous. I finally get a modicum of control over one curse, then I'm hit with another.

While more people in scrubs rushed in and attempted to haul Tucker onto a stretcher, he fought them off. "I'm fine. I just need some water and something to eat."

I couldn't hide my relief and tears dripped down my face unbidden. I didn't hurt him permanently. To think of Tucker lying in bed, delusional or in a coma like the other people in this ward. Wait. The Wasting. Was it caused from Heidi recovering? The vision with Forrest and Michelle in the alley showed me Heidi seemingly sleeping next to the homeless man we found the next day who turned out to have the disease. Holy shit, that was what Forrest was hiding. He was using high risk victims to recharge his money maker so he could do more shows. Forrest couldn't cure Heidi. She was not lying to me when I'd questioned her, I was sure of that. Which meant she didn't know. I had to get out of here.

Chapter Twenty-Five

When I tried to flag down a nurse to get these things out of my arms, I relished the renewed strength pulsing in my muscles. Tucker was being guided away from the ward, hopefully to get something to eat, when Flores rushed in. They stopped and spoke for a moment, then Tucker waved weakly at me and allowed himself to be led out.

Flores reached down to grab my hand, but I yanked it away before we touched. "Don't. There's something going on I can't fully explain, but I need to get out of here now."

"That's not happening." He crossed his arms and shook his head like he was disappointed. But the tingling in my fingers and toes told me he was happy, really truly happy. "You were in a coma. Tucker texted me as soon as you woke up."

Oh great, my partner and my boyfriend were not only on a first name basis, they texted each other too. "I know what's going on with this Wasting sickness." I sat up and folded my legs under me, relishing the lack of tension in my foot. "Forrest is using—"

He interrupted me. "How did you do it? You told me you couldn't heal."

"I couldn't. Pedro was my first attempt and I have no idea

exactly what I did or how I knew I could do it." I couldn't help but smile. It felt really good to heal someone and bring a bit of peace to Flores. No wonder Heidi risked so much of her own well-being to help others. I could see it becoming addictive. "How is he?"

Flores sat down in the chair Tucker had recently vacated. "He's doing amazingly well. He's actually just down the hallway. They can't find any tumors in the MRI. They're calling it a miracle." He leaned over me but didn't touch me. "You're a miracle."

I rubbed the tears from my cheeks with two open palms. "If only I could heal someone without going into a coma."

Flores cocked his head. "How does Heidi do it?"

This no-nonsense detective so readily accepting these supernatural occurrences gave me hope that maybe, just maybe, Tucker would understand as well. "I'm not sure you're going to like that answer. But it has a lot to do with why I needed you to not touch me. I'm afraid I almost added Tucker to the Wasting patient list."

Flores's furrowed brow told me he was trying to put two and two together.

I wasn't sure I had it right either. "Can we try something? I can't promise that it will be safe."

Without hesitation, Flores scooted the chair closer and put his hands on the railing. "Whatever you need."

I needed to get out of the hospital to get some questions answered, but I couldn't risk the orderlies touching me if I was going to weaken them. Heidi had said I touched her before she was prepared and that she'd pushed Forrest away because she hadn't been prepared to be touched yet. Which meant there was a way to block the transfer, it wasn't totally out of my control. I just had to figure out how.

Tentatively, I touched Flores's hand with the tip of my finger. The warmth, just like with Tucker flowed into my hand and quickly climbed my arm, but not as lightning fast as before. If I had to guess, I'd say it was because I was stronger this time.

When I'd healed Pedro, I was able to poor my energy into him. It stood to reason I could use my energy to block another's, just like I use my own emotions as a barricade.

I still wasn't at 100 percent, but I wasn't weak anymore either. So I closed my eyes and traveled within, finding the energy that was me, my own spark. With a gentle push, it flowed through my shoulder, stopping Flores's from going any deeper. Then I propelled the warmth down my arm and through my finger back into Flores, stopping before I flooded him with my not limitless strength. This entire interaction sapped a bit more of my control. I needed to put up a barrier until I was back to normal.

I hoped so anyway. I'd just gotten the ability to walk around without gloves and actually touch people. If this new manifestation took that away from me, I just might rebel.

I removed my finger and studied Flores's face for a reaction. "How do you feel?"

He stood up and stretched as if testing his body. "Normal. Though a bit sore, but I think that has more to do with sleeping in a hospital chair than anything that happened just now."

"Thank you for being my guinea pig."

Flores leaned down in that protective way that made me feel safe. "I need you healthy so you can help me find the real killer and clear Pedro's name."

I laughed. "Of course, Detective. I'll be back on the case in no time. Meanwhile, can you grab my clothes?" I waved over someone in scrubs, at this point I wasn't sure what his actual job was. "I'm ready to sign myself out. I want some real food and a shower."

He looked nervous. "I don't think Dr. Fountain would approve of you leaving so soon." He took a moment to take in my physical appearance which I knew very well was much healthier than a few minutes ago. "Especially with your quick recovery. You might have the key to helping the rest of these patients."

I swung my legs over the side of the bed where Flores had pulled down my railing.

The nurse or whatever he was rushed out the door calling Dr. Fountain's name.

Flores pulled out a plastic bag from under the bed. "These must be yours."

When he placed them beside me, I saw I still had Heidi's shoes. "Heidi's shoes," I said out loud.

I remembered her on stage wearing peach shoes. Michelle had done something to me that made me forget, something I couldn't explain. I shuttered to think what would have happened if the Collected hadn't shown up. "Oh, Flores, I forgot about the shoes. I can't prove it right now, but I'm sure I could if I got to touch them. Heidi wore a pair of shoes identical to the one Henrietta had when Tucker and I spoke to her, the one she claimed the Shadow dropped. What if it had dropped off her foot when she was downtown and Henrietta had been murdered to get it back?"

Flores's face darkened as he reached into his pocket for his phone to start taking notes. "Why would Heidi have been in that part of town? I thought she healed from the stage."

I motioned to the ward of Wasting patients. "I know why they're like this. Forrest has convinced Heidi that he has some sort of ability that recharges her healing energy faster than she could recover on her own. And, technically, he's not lying. He uses the indigent population that comes to him for help to recharge Heidi."

Absently rubbing the top of his hand where I'd touched him, he asked while looking at the Wasting patients. "That's what you were testing with me."

"Yep. I'm afraid I took some energy from Tucker inadvertently. Not enough to make him sick, at least I hope not." Could Heidi heal him if I made him sick? Could I? Could the people in this ward be healed by either of us? So much to learn. "I couldn't keep going until I learned to control it. So thanks for being a guinea pig."

"Then how is Forrest tricking Heidi if she can control it?"

Dr. Fountain walked in with a look on her face that spoke of her disapproval before she opened her mouth.

I answered Flores before I started the heated argument I was about to have with the doctor. "That's a good question. You should ask him about it while I get dressed." Defiantly, I jumped off the bed to show Dr. Fountain how strong I was.

Flores's lip ticked up just a bit. As he headed for the exit, he offered Dr. Fountain a bit of advice. "I've worked with Fauna for over a year now. If I was you, I wouldn't argue. It's a waste of breath."

Unsure whether to be flattered or offended, I yanked my pants on under the hospital gown. "Don't you have bad guys to arrest or something?"

"See," Flores said as the door closed behind him.

I held my arm up for Nurse Michael who seemed to be attached to Dr. Fountain's hip. "Either take these out or I'm doing it."

Dr. Fountain stopped blinking at me and finally spoke up. "I have to do some tests to determine how you bounced back so quickly. Your symptoms were the same as these other patients, if not more severe since only a couple are in a coma. Whatever worked for you, might work for the rest of them."

A momentary bout of guilt about abandoning the Wasting patients stopped my forward movement. No, I was not responsible for all of society, and I refused to put everyone's pain and illness on my shoulders. I didn't cause this suffering. Forrest had. I had to be there when Flores confronted him. I might not be able to sense his emotions, but I knew him better than I knew myself. I could help.

In response to Dr. Fountain's pleading, I reached up to the plastic tube stuck in my arm. "There's about to be some blood on your spotless floor."

"Stop it." Tucker pushed through the door looking much better than when he'd left. Well, that was fast. Did he have powers too? As the swinging doors pushed one way a bit too hard, I noticed Heidi on the other side talking to Flores. When did she get here? I was missing out on so much stuck in this stupid hospital.

Tucker gently pushed me down on the bed. "I'm her doctor and I'm signing her out." He waved over the nurse who didn't argue and immediately turned off the beeping machines and pulled everything out of my skin. I couldn't take my eyes off of Tucker. This take control aspect of him was super sexy.

Once I was free, Tucker closed the privacy curtain. He argued with Dr. Fountain while I got decent as quickly as I could, silently grateful there was no mirror because I couldn't imagine what state my hair and make-up were in. Tucker handed me my phone as soon as I left the curtains and escorted me to the exit. Dr. Fountain fumed behind us. Her anger gripped my gut, but I didn't stop walking.

I looked up at Tucker. "You're not going to get in trouble for this, are you?"

When he held the door open and Heidi smiled up at him, I was surprised by the animal inside that almost made me growl out loud. I couldn't help but brush Tucker's exposed elbow to get a reading. No flush of lust or any deep emotions came across. With a deep breath, I told my heart to calm the fuck down. Since when did I feel jealousy anyway?

I asked, "Where did Flores go?"

Heidi answered, her voice not at full strength. "Detective Flores went to find Forrest. He disappeared and I thought maybe he came to visit you in the hospital. The detective said ..." She trailed off as she looked with wide eyes at Tucker and pleading ones at me.

Then I noticed that Heidi leaned against the wall heavily instead of casually. Oh, I knew what happened. "Tucker, Flores was supposed to call Amelia to pick me up. Could you make sure she can get into the waiting room for us?"

"I can. I can do whatever you need. I'm just grateful you're on your feet." He leaned down and very unprofessionally kissed me.

A gentle warmth flowed through my skin and swelled in my chest. I almost pulled away afraid I was taking energy from him again until I recognized the emotion. It was love.

Chapter Twenty-Six

Before I had time to freak out over that revelation, Heidi's anger made my jaw tighten. What did I do to her?

She didn't make me guess. "Why didn't you tell me you were a healer too?"

"Because I'm not—well wasn't—a healer. I've never had the ability."

Heidi pushed up from the wall a bit too quickly and stumbled. Instinctively, I reached out and caught her. Though I could sense her anger loud and clear, I didn't *feel* her energy. She had her barriers up.

I sighed in frustration when she pulled away from me. "Flores said you healed his cousin, the one Austin was trying to get me to go see. And I saw Dr. Wickman ambling down the hallway, his soul obviously weakened. Did you do that to him?"

She could recognize what happened just by looking? "This is a hospital. How could you tell what was wrong?"

"Oh, so you don't deny using him as your own personal battery?" Heidi shook her head and looked away like she couldn't bear to meet my eyes.

"No," I protested, "not exactly. I didn't know what was

happening when I woke up and found myself in the hospital." She wasn't going to believe me. But if she recognized the symptoms once, maybe she would recognize them again. "As Forrest's sister, will you give me one more chance to show you?"

A tear dripped down her face and her anger faded. "Do you know where he is?"

"I don't, but Detective Flores will find him."

An eye twitch joined my aching jaw. She was worried about him. I was about to shatter everything she believed about my brother. Yeah, I was definitely not a healer, but I couldn't let Heidi continue to live like this. If what Tucker said was correct, and those other cities had these cases before Houston, the trail of Wasting followed Heidi and Forrest. Heidi didn't want to hurt anyone. I could feel it deep down. Based on how upset she got when she thought I'd used Tucker as my own personal battery, she'd be devastated when she found out how many she'd weakened.

It was now or never. "Please, come with me."

I took Heidi's hand without a rush of energy or emotions. My own were so flared up, nothing else could have gotten through unless I allowed it.

Dr. Fountain confronted me as soon as we entered. "What are you doing back? And who is—"

I interrupted her before she drove us away. "You were right, Dr. Fountain, and I was being totally selfish. I'll gladly give you blood and whatever else you need for your tests."

While we talked, Heidi noticed the patients and walked around me.

Relief loosened the doctor's tight muscles. "Thank you, Ms. Young. I just want to help these patients. You could be the key."

I totally was the key, just not in the way she imagined.

"But I'm afraid your friend can't stay."

Time to turn on the con artist charm. "Oh please let her stay. Dr. Wickman brought her back here to convince me to do the right thing. If it wasn't for my friend, I wouldn't even consider this course. She made me see it was only right of me to help others. I don't think I could go through it without her."

Heidi didn't say a word when Dr. Fountain turned to her. The healer's focus never left the Wasting patients. There was at least a dozen, and I couldn't imagine what she was feeling right now. More victims produced by an empath guided down the wrong road by my brother. He really did need to be stopped before he found someone new to manipulate.

"Okay, fine. We still haven't found the means of contagion yet. So keep her by your side and away from everyone else." Dr. Fountain nodded to Nurse Michael who really did worship her, I could feel it. I tried to wipe the picture of Dr. Frankstein and Igor from my head. But I truly needed the delightful image before I shattered Heidi's life.

As soon as the doctor left, Heidi and I rushed over to the nearest bed.

She looked at me in horror. "What did you do to these people?"

Okay, I didn't expect that reaction. "It wasn't me, Heidi." I swallowed deeply. "It was you."

Her brows furrowed and she tapped her hip with her hand. "That's ridiculous. I've never seen any of these people before. And I swore I'd never sap one person to heal another. I'm not God. I won't make choices like that."

Fuck, this is much harder than it should be. Damn you, Forrest. "You know how you think Forrest recharges you somehow without succumbing to," I gestured across the ward, "this?"

"I know it's unusual, but considering what I can do and what you can do, why don't you believe your brother? He's helped so many. Why can't you see that he's changed from when he was with you?"

A glance toward the door told me I didn't have much time as Nurse Michael came in with a tray of needles and vials. "Look. He does repower you quicker than your body can naturally handle, because he uses these people to do it. I saw you in an impression, a memory left by Forrest, and you were passed out beside this man. The next day, we found the same man at the scene of a murder with the Wasting sickness."

She shook her head. She fought me with everything she had. "I've never seen this man before in my life."

The truth was painful. That I could completely relate to. I had to try another tactic. "How does Forrest do what he does? Like what exactly happens step by step."

Heidi moved to another bed and cocked her head at the patient, a young woman with blotchy skin who mumbled about shadows but didn't look us in the eyes. "After a healing session, he makes me my tea to quiet my screaming muscles and weakened soul. You saw him do that after I healed you."

Was that regret in her tone? No time to get distracted. "And then what happens?"

For the first time, Heidi looked at me with doubt. "I fall asleep and in the morning I'm back to 100 percent."

"So you never actually watch Forrest recharge you, share his soul energy, or whatever you were calling it, with you?"

She flung her arms out and my gut clenched at the same time as my throat clenched almost completely shut. Her frustration and rage were so strong it busted through everything even when I hadn't touched her. "Look. Forrest wouldn't do this. He wants to help people too. We're on the same page."

I walked away to give myself some distance so I could breathe again. Now I was angry. "Denial's a bitch, Heidi. You can't run from the truth. It always finds you." Like Sylvia's death.

A man's voice got my attention from the bed next to me. "Is that the Healer? Can she help me. Please." The last word faded as his head fell back on his pillow, seemingly too weak to pick it up again.

He looked familiar, like a faded memory. Then he hummed "I Could Fall in Love" and I almost fell down. It was that man Michelle brought to Heidi after she'd healed me.

"Heidi, do you remember this man?"

She stomped over, like she just couldn't take my bullshit anymore. I knew the feeling. "Why would I ... Wait. That's Riko Hernandez. I met him a few days ago. He was trying to get us to help his sister, but Michelle assured us his sister had already passed and the poor man was delusional." Her anger dropped off as she spoke to the bedridden man. "Mr. Hernandez, what happened?"

He blinked his eyes open. I remembered them being a deep brown, but right now they appeared speckled with gray. "Healer? You're back. I knew you would return after I freely gave what you need to heal my sister. Where is she? I want to tell her I love her and I'm sorry."

Without hesitation, Heidi grasped his limp hand in her own. She looked up at me with tears in her eyes. "Do you know what soul sickness looks like?"

"I know what sick souls look like."

She tried to smile, but it was as if her face didn't have the strength to lift. She grabbed my hand and my chest hollowed out, like someone had scooped out all of my confidence. Shit, Heidi. She carried guilt much more heavily than I ever had. But I forgot everything else when she put my hand between hers and Riko's. He felt more than hollow; he felt empty without enough energy left for any emotion.

When I tried to yank my hand away, Heidi held it there with unexpected strength. "No," she said. "If you're going to heal people, you need to know what happens if you don't control your own recovery."

I couldn't argue with that, so I quit struggling. "Fair. Show me."

"Do you see that vermillion hue around his organs?"

"No." I didn't see anything. I only felt the emptiness.

Heidi seemed surprised. "Look closer. Maybe you don't know what you're seeing, but it's there. It's like a fog over the organs that beats in time to his heart."

As she continued to describe what I should be seeing, a haze blurred along where his organs would be in his abdomen. It outlined them instead of showing up in glowing yellow spots like Pedro's cancer had. I swore there was nothing there before Heidi described it. I couldn't see inside of him like an MRI. There were no details, but if I let my eyes lose focus, there was a definite pattern of dull red encircling each organ. Out of curiosity, I scanned up to his brain. The same pulsating haze encircled it as well.

"What is that?" I asked.

This time Heidi did smile. "Good. You do see it. That's what Dr. Wickman looked like when I saw him, only not so severe." She gestured around the room. "Some of these patients are much, much worse. I don't know how they have the energy to continue to breathe."

With my newfound sight, I looked at the other patients and gasped. All of them had some level of deep red haze covering vital organs. "Will they recover?"

She shrugged. "I've never seen anything like this before."

"Fauna."

At the sound of my name, I looked toward the door and held myself as I saw Tucker and realized what I'd done to him. He looked good now. No sign of hazy organs or anything harmful like that. "Can you heal them like you did Tucker, er, Dr. Wickman?"

After taking a long deep breath, she nodded slowly, her whole upper body rocking with the movement. "With your help and some time, yes. But you have to promise me never to do anything like this again."

Shock rocked me back a step. "I couldn't even heal before yesterday. Some of these patients have been in here for days. I didn't do this, Heidi. You did."

Her anger flashed back up again. "And I thought we were getting somewhere."

My frustration added to the seething mix. If only she could feel emotions like I could heal, we'd be on the same page. "Look.

You didn't do it on purpose. Forrest orchestrated the whole thing. He doesn't have any special ability. He just figured out the trick to yours and invented a way to take advantage of it. It's what he does. It's what he always does."

"Forrest would never do this to another human being. And he would certainly not involve me in causing another person's pain. He knows what it means to me."

Tucker interrupted our fight. "Fauna, I'm so happy you agreed to take some tests to help us help these people. Should I tell Amelia to go home? I could always give you a ride when we're done here."

It was time to bring out the big guns. Heidi didn't believe me. Her dependence on Forrest for purpose and some semblance of safety clouded any logical thinking about what she was actually seeing. That had been me a few years ago. I understood her position more than she could imagine. I had to prove it to her to save her.

"Dr. Wickman, when did the first Wasting patient show up in the ER?"

After recovering from the shock of me calling him Dr. Wickman, Tucker replied, "Eight days ago."

I turned to Heidi who had her arms closed and wouldn't look at me. "When did you get to town?"

She sighed, like she was humoring a child. "Eight days ago, but that's just a coincidence."

Without losing Heidi's gaze, I asked Tucker another question. "And which city did this disease pop up in before Houston?"

Tucker seemed confused at the import of my questions but thank god he just answered. "Dallas had six cases."

Heidi's confident stance faltered, but she didn't say anything.

I mouthed to Tucker *I'll explain later,* then asked him, "And the one before that?"

"Shreveport," he said.

I prompted. "And then?"

Tucker and Heidi said at the same time, "Little Rock."

"Those are the cities we toured, in order." Reality struck and Heidi leaned on Riko's bed. "How could he?"

Tucker looked confused but seemed comfortable enough with it to not question me now. "So, Fauna, the blood tests?"

The not patient anymore nurse gestured to my empty bed like he invited me to a fancy gala.

"About that, I've got to find my brother before he skips town."

Tucker's disappointment made my eyes burn. After he'd given me so much trust, I was going to walk out on him. Again. "I can't make you stay."

His thought hinted at a *but*. If only I could tell him that more tests would do no good and that Heidi and I could help all of these patients, it would just take time. I clung to his chest and reached up on my tiptoes so I could get as close to his gorgeous eyes as possible. He instinctively wrapped his arms around my waist and bent his head down. Dammit, that warmth again. And this time I wasn't sure where his love stopped and mine began. I loved this man. What was I supposed to do with that?

Instead, I offered him a promise. "Look. I know this is a lot to take in and it seems like I'm being selfish, but I assure you that Heidi and I can help these patients, it will just take time."

Heidi backed me up. "I'm not going anywhere until they're all on their feet again."

Tucker leaned down and pecked my lips. "I'm choosing to trust you because I don't think I could handle any other outcome. But I do expect an explanation."

"I have a doozy of an explanation." I swallowed hard, as the lump in my throat threatened to stop any more talk. "But I can prove it, after I make sure my brother can't hurt anyone else."

Chapter Twenty-Seven

Amelia dropped me off at my townhouse while she ran to get us some breakfast. I don't know what I'd do without her. As soon as I touched my door handle to put my key in, that familiar signature drifted up from the door. Had Forrest been here? No, it wasn't him. I was sure of it by this point. But I'd felt the same thing before Michelle popped beside me, and I swore she hadn't been there a moment before. Was she leaving these odd feelings of familiarity? But she had been in the trailer and I didn't feel it in there for anyone. It couldn't be Heidi. We'd left her in the hospital. Plus, I'd never met her until recently. She couldn't be causing this familiar sensation.

With a shake of my head, I decided to leave the conundrum until I found Forrest. For a moment, I thought the sensation followed me inside, but then it was gone. Even if it had been Michelle and even if she did have nefarious intent, she couldn't have made it inside. The door was locked just like I'd left it.

As I passed by the fridge, I grabbed a bottle of white and a glass. I'd earned it. I could heal now. What was I supposed to do with that? Suddenly, I needed the Collected. Had anyone else experienced this before? I wasn't sure where to put it, like I already had to block other's emotions with my own, how was I going to block their illnesses too. Every time someone had a cold and I touched them, would I black out? I should have been nicer to Heidi, maybe she'd help me figure it all out. She didn't exactly live a normal life, but that was already off the table for me.

I threw down my first glass of wine like it was a shot. I set the bottle on my vanity and turned on the shower to get hot. It wouldn't take long in the Houston summer. When I stepped back into my bedroom to grab clean underwear, that odd experience washed over me like steam from the shower. I froze.

"You can sense me, can't you?" Michelle's voice, but where was she?

I turned around slowly, scanning my surroundings. How could I have missed her? My room wasn't that big. From the corner by my bed, a shadow moved. My stomach turned as I realized what I'd seen beside the trailer before Michelle appeared. "How are you doing that?"

Michelle stepped around the bed, becoming solid as she moved. "I'm not really sure. How do you know what people are feeling? How does Heidi heal?" She shrugged.

"It was you leaving those impressions all over town. Whatever that shadow thing is you're doing must be what I was sensing." I don't know why I was afraid. It was just Michelle. What was she going to do? List her grievances? That was what she normally did. "How did you get in here?"

She set down a key on my dresser. "You never changed your locks. Probably not smart when you break up a perfectly good thing because you feel guilty for no reason whatsoever."

Well, I'd fix that first thing tomorrow. "It was for a very good reason. Sylvia Remington killed herself because of the lies we told her. I told her. I started to imagine much more horror in my wake instead of healing as Forrest always said we were doing."

Michelle laughed. A genuine, full belly laugh. I'd never heard so much as a giggle from her when we traveled together. Whatever she was feeling though, it wasn't joy. My fingers and toes remained untickled. "Sylvia was way too egotistical to kill herself.

That woman thought the world revolved around her because she had money. After she got the call from her daughter, she contacted me and threatened to sue Forrest for the damage he'd caused. Damage? What damage? Stupid bitch. No one threatens Forrest."

My shock prevented me from diving deeper into Michelle's emotional state. "You knew about the daughter? Sylvia called you? Why didn't you tell us?"

She got closer to me and pushed my out-of-control hair back from my forehead. "Why would I tell you? My job is to protect Forrest. And anyone who threatens to harm him must be dealt with."

As her skin touched mine, my shoulder muscles burned as if I'd just lifted a boulder over my head. She really hated me, like deeply and truly. I didn't know why, but I was in danger. I backed up into my bathroom to swing the door closed, but she grabbed my wrist and pulled it toward her so my forearm slammed in the door jamb. Pain bloomed at the site of impact, and I instinctively yanked my arm back, which pulled Michelle into the bathroom with me. Fuck, her grip was like iron and my throbbing forearm added to the pain in my shoulders. I'd walked into my home feeling safe and didn't have any of my barriers up. If I could keep her talking, maybe I'd have time to get them all in order. Hopefully, the fatigue from the hospital didn't make it impossible.

Time to trust a hunch and buy some time. "How was killing Henrietta protecting Forrest, especially when he saw the dead body? That sweet old lady didn't have any power to harm anyone."

Michelle released my wrist and poured me a glass of wine. "Well, I didn't know her name, but that homeless bitch had one of Heidi's shoes. I have no idea how she got it, but I couldn't let her walk around with it and she refused to let it go."

"So you killed her?" I took a sip of wine to stop my body from shaking while I gathered my growing anger at Michelle into a physical barrier around my body. "You're the shadow she talked about. She saw you."

"Forrest had to get Heidi downtown without being seen. I had a way to do that."

With a long drag of my wine, I put more pieces together. "An angel carried by a demon, one of the victims had said. That was Forrest carrying Heidi."

Michelle smirked as she reached over to turn off the shower. "Wouldn't you rather have a bath?"

As the water filled up the tub, the thought of Sylvia lying in hers, dead, for her daughter to find infuriated me. "You killed the volunteer from St. Benedict's too?"

When I set down the glass a bit too aggressively on the vanity, Michelle looked up. "He was recognizing the pattern and came to see one of our shows and followed us when Forrest found a new battery." She dropped a bath bomb in the water and soothing lavender filled the air. It would never calm me again. "You know he killed himself though, right? There's no murder to investigate no matter how much you fancy yourself a detective now. Same with the old rich lady and the old homeless one."

I rubbed my hand over my face. I should have been more scared, but this wasn't the first time I'd been stuck in a small space with a psychopath. I could handle myself. I had one more vital question. "If you were intent on ending these people, why do you fake suicides? Wouldn't it be easier to just shoot them?"

"People don't ask questions when it's a suicide." Michelle leaned against the vanity with her arms crossed, imitating my stance to a tee. "Well, most people don't."

She pulled out a silver blade that looked like it came out of someone's fine dining steak knife set. Delicate roses, thorns and all, were carved into the handle, reminding me of the beloved rose bushes on the Remington estate.

"They do ask questions when no murder weapon is left behind," I said.

Michelle tilted her head, seeming to consider what I'd said

THE HEALER

instead of having all the answers as she had for the rest of our conversation. "It was a mistake to take the knife from the Remington estate. But it was so pretty, and it represented my personal power. I just couldn't let it go. I suppose I don't need this symbol anymore. If I leave it here, I'm sure your little detective will put the pieces together. You killed all those people and then yourself because you couldn't handle the guilt any longer." She waved her hand up and down. "Now if you'd kindly disrobe."

I needed to take her down before Amelia came back with breakfast. I didn't need her in the middle of this. "Are you mad? Why would I do anything you asked me to do?"

Michelle shrugged. "That's fine. I prefer the hard way."

Her hands shot out and wrapped around my head. Nope. I was ready this time. I grabbed hold of her wrists and squeezed my eyes shut as I poured the memory of my torture at the hands of the serial killer Phil Tanner into Michelle's mind, starting with the knife in my shoulder.

One of her arms dropped from my face as she yelped more in surprise than pain. "What are you doing?"

"Giving you a taste." I renewed my assault sending through the agony of an impaled foot. Mine might be healed, but the memory of the pain never went away completely.

Michelle fell to her knee as her foot gave out. Her grip on the other side of my face was so strong, I fell with her. "No!" she yelled.

I almost had her. Time for the gut punch, literally. When I searched for my slashed and mutilated abdomen to share with Michelle, I couldn't find it. My energy level dropped, and I felt the uncontrollable need to lie down.

Michelle's heavy breathing over me should have sent me into a panic. My heart swelled for a moment as Michelle's triumph overcame my determination. I thought about sitting up and fighting more but decided that was just too much effort. I was so tired, and I deserved some peace.

As Michelle lifted me, she spoke in a sing-song voice like a mother to her baby. I found it oddly comforting and closed my eyes. "There we go. That's better. You had me worried there for a second."

When she placed me in the hot bath water, a jolt of awareness washed away the peaceful feeling. "Wait." My voice was raspy, like I was waking up from a long sleep.

"Shhhh," Michelle touched both of my cheeks and my mind quieted in a way I could never get it to do on my own. My worries faded, and all I wanted to do was take a long, peaceful nap.

A scrape of metal on stone attracted my sleepy attention, but it didn't awaken any alarms. I was at home wrapped in warm water, relaxing for the first time in a long time. I should do this more often. Maybe after Flores arrested my brother, I could take a break. That was enough emotional baggage for anyone, especially an empath, right?

Michelle knelt beside the bathtub. I'd forgotten she was there. She should probably go. She'd be pissed when she found out about her unrequited love's imminent imprisonment. "Hey, Michelle," my voice sounded so far away, "thanks for the bath. But don't let me keep you. Deteg, nope, Detetiff, huh uh, Florrest." How much wine had I drank? "The hot cop has search permission for RV. That brother of mine will have to face some music. Oh, can you turn on my Spotify?"

Michelle's anger tightened my gut, killing my high. "I'll deal with that damn detective next."

At the hint of Flores in danger, whatever she was doing to sooth me faded enough that I could form full thoughts again. When she pulled my arm from the water and placed the cold blade against my warm skin, my fight returned to me. These were the last moments of Sylvia's life. She laid in her bathtub thinking about her daughter returning while Michelle sliced her wrists.

"No!" I yelled to my quiet mind just as much as to what

THE HEALER

Michelle was about to do. As I pulled my arm back, she dropped the knife and water sloshed over the floor.

She growled. "Stop fighting me. If you just give in, you won't feel a thing. And then all of your pain will be over."

She might have dropped the knife, but her grip on my wrist didn't waver and her soothing energy threatened to end all of my fighting. Dammit, I wasn't going out with a whimper, but I was too weak to fight. The last twenty-four hours had worn down my ability to the point that I didn't know Michelle was in my apartment until she let me see her.

But I could get more energy now. Healing had a reverse side: weakening. Sure, it happened on accident the first time I'd touched Tucker, but I experienced the transfer precisely when I tested this new skill with Flores. I was sure I could sap Michelle of this abundance she seemed to possess.

Rolling to my side with much more effort than it should have taken, I grasped Michelle's hand that was wrapped around my other wrist. She searched the floor for the knife and didn't seem overly concerned with my movement. My internal energy, the uniqueness that made up me, bounced with excitement as it sucked on Michelle's energy like a baby on a midnight bottle. Better than the most crafted drink, better than fresh-made crusty bed, better than sex, this high drove me to want more.

Michelle looked up in shock. "What are you doing?" Her panic penetrated my fingers but didn't go any further because any space I had for emotions was eaten up by the flow of Michelle's life energy. It felt so good.

She grabbed me with her other hand and tried to push the soothing into me. It was wasted effort and only served to weaken her more. Why would Heidi ever stop doing this? I sat up in the bathtub feeling better than I'd ever felt in my life. Michele had resorted to attempting to peel back my fingers from her skin, but her strength had ebbed so dramatically she slumped against the floor.

She blinked up at me and I swore her eyes were two shades darker. "Please, stop."

I scoffed. "You don't like being the helpless one, do you?" My very muscles vibrated. I felt like a superhero. For about a second and a half, I was sure I could fly. If I drained the last bit from her, I could very well be immortal. She deserved it, right? She killed so many innocents. This was justice.

With a deep inhale, Michelle's energy poured into me like oxygen. And I felt like a god.

Chapter Twenty-Eight

The bathroom door slammed against the wall and strong hands pried us apart before I realized we weren't alone.

My brother's voice, though it sounded far away through the buzzing in my ears, shouted, "Leave her alone, Michelle! She's my sister."

Amelia rushed in right after him. She grabbed my shoulders. "Oh, Fauna, you're soaked. Let's get you out of here."

Her green eyes and bouncy hair made me giggle. She looked like a cartoon character with her skin glowing in that weird way. I wondered what her energy felt like. With a slight pull, I got a taste.

"Fauna?" Surprise filled Amelia's eyes, but I didn't feel it in my bones at all.

Suddenly, everything felt unnatural. I pushed Amelia back from me. "Don't touch me."

I leaned on the bathtub finally feeling the weight of my wet clothes hanging from my body. On the floor, Forrest's tone changed from admonishing Michelle to concern for her. I didn't blame him. She didn't look good. Her skin was pale-yellow and her eyes, though open, were sunk in her face. Her chest still moved up and down, but the sound was raspy and rattled as if it would completely breakdown at any moment. I still felt so damn good, the contrast was striking.

Then it hit me. I felt so damn good because I'd drained most of Michelle's life energy. I'd gone from an empath to a fledgling healer to a succubus. What the fuck was happening to me? Even though Michelle had killed those people, I didn't have the right to be executioner. "Forrest." My voice had never sounded so commanding. "Let me get closer."

My clothes offered no hindrance as I gracefully jumped from the tub and landed on solid footing, even with the slippery tile. I really did feel like a superhero. My head shook as the rational side of my brain tried to maintain control. It wasn't easy with this power coursing through my system.

Forrest blinked up at me, tears streaming down his cheeks. "Did you do this?"

My instinct was self-defense. "She was about to slice my wrists." Guilt dampened my high and kept me moving in the right direction. "But, yes, I did do this. I can fix it, I think."

As Michelle laid in my brother's arms like she'd probably always dreamed about, she blinked up at him. "I only ever protected you."

Pity took over from self-righteousness. Michelle was really another victim of my brother's.

Forrest rubbed her wan cheek. "I know."

Did he? Had he known she was murdering people who threatened his con? Before my anger took over and I made more bad decisions, I flattened my palm on Michelle's chest. The pulsing vermillion haze surrounding her organs was thick and viscous. Her heartbeat was so weak I wouldn't have been able to feel it if every cell in my body wasn't supercharged. Well, they wouldn't be for long. I took a deep breath, closed my eyes, and pushed. Energy flowed out of me, slowly at first, but then it accelerated as Michelle's hungry body drank up. My high faded and my thoughts became easier to control again. The real question became when do I stop?

Before I drained myself too far, I opened my eyes and watched Michelle's health return. Her skin regained its healthy color and the skin around her eyes plumped out. Most importantly, the red glow around her organs dissipated. When her heart beat strong and true under my hand, I sat back, cutting off contact.

Michelle inhaled deeply like she'd just breached the surface after a deep dive.

The bathtub's water faucet turned off, dropping the bathroom that had been chaos just moments before into silence. Amelia handed me a towel which I gratefully accepted. When I reached up to squeeze her hand in thank you, she yanked it away and took a step back. My stomach lurched with her fear, and my guilt doubled. After making so much headway, I'd just terrified my most loyal friend. I had no idea how I would make it up to her.

As I towel dried my hair—ignoring the problem would make it go away, right?—a knock on my bedroom door turned all of our heads.

I felt Flores's concern before Amelia stepped back and Flores stuck his head into the bathroom. "Fauna? Your door was open."

By the movement of his hands, I guessed he was holstering his gun. I remembered the last time he saved me. At least, I didn't make him kill anyone this time. Though I almost had. What had happened to my life?

Flores stood straight up as he recognized who was in the bathroom with me. "I've been looking for you," he said to Forrest.

Michelle pulled Forrest down and kissed him. My brother's arms flew out on either side, his shock imminent though my abilities retained their blind spot for his emotions. Michelle's, however, were blatantly obvious. My body filled with warmth even as I felt it hard to breathe. That mix of love and sadness emanated from her, and I wished Forrest could feel it too. I wished he knew what he did to the people around him in this visceral way. Maybe, he'd change.

Amelia whistled, which made me feel much better than it should have. It meant she still had her sense of humor. I hadn't robbed her of anything permanent, I hoped anyway. I didn't pick up any haze around her organs. That would have to satisfy me for now.

After releasing Forrest, Michelle stood up with more energy than one would expect from someone who had been at death's door moments ago. "I did it. I killed all those people. Forrest had nothing to do with it. He didn't even know I was doing it. The murder weapon is right there." She pointed to the silver knife in a puddle on the tile floor.

So she was protecting Forrest one last time. I'd never loved anyone like that. If she was innocent, I might have protested. But she had killed all those people. Regardless of who she did it for, she did pull the trigger or utilize the knife or some equally horrifying saying.

Flores tilted his head at me, and I simply nodded the truth of the confession.

From the floor, Forrest stared up at Michelle with his mouth wide open. "What are you talking about? What people? You murdered someone?"

While Flores read Michelle her rights and put her in hand cuffs, I took pity on my brother. "Sylvia's suicide wasn't a suicide."

His face flushed. "How long have you known?"

"I just learned about it a few days ago. And there are more."

I offered him a hand and he took it. Easier than it should have been, I helped him gain his feet.

For maybe the first time ever, Forrest really looked at me. "What happened to you, Fauna? You're different."

"I wish I knew," I replied, too tired to be witty. "Though you haven't changed at all."

Forrest's anger flared. "That's completely untrue and unfair. I help people now, for real."

I wanted to scream at him that helping people who can pay and then making those who can't ill wasn't helping people. "I know you conned Heidi into traveling with you with a fake head injury."

"The injury wasn't fake." My glare seemed to pull a few more words from him. "Michelle hit me pretty hard with a baseball bat. I couldn't test Heidi's abilities on a fake injury."

"But they didn't work on you."

"Nope, just like yours don't work on me."

So that's why he was able to pull Michelle and I apart even though we were flinging our abilities around willy-nilly. I chanced a quick glance at Amelia who turned away as soon as our eyes met. And yet more wrongs I had to put right.

Forrest said, "I need to go find Heidi. That's why I came here to begin with. I thought maybe she was with you. She said something about needing to talk to you."

I could have stopped him, but it was up to Heidi to confront him about what he did to her, what he made her do. That didn't mean I couldn't make him sweat a little. "She's at the hospital healing patients who've come down with some sort of Wasting sickness of unknown origin."

Forrest's eyes widened in fear, and he rushed out the door.

As my brother flew past Flores, the detective asked, "Why do I feel like I should arrest him too?"

Amelia folded her arms at his retreat. "That's because you have good instincts."

"But I'm afraid what he's guilty of can't be proven in a mundane court of law." I fell on my bed, then bounced right back up as my sopping wet clothes contrasted with my dry bedding. I needed to get out of those. "Can I kick y'all out so I can change?"

Without fighting me at all, Amelia immediately moved toward the kitchen. Dammit, I'd really freaked her out.

Flores, however, shook his head. "I'm afraid you can't change yet. Pradock is coming to photograph the scene and collect the evidence."

"Of course, I'm evidence again." I picked up my brush from the dresser and tried to work out the wet knots. "At least, I'm conscious this time."

Flores chuckled. "That is an improvement."

"Um, Fauna?" Amelia held my phone up. I hadn't even heard it ring. "It's your brother." Realizing she should probably specify, she added, "Sparrow."

What odd timing. We hadn't talked since Christmas and he calls when Forrest was just here? "Tell him I'll call back later."

"He said it's important. Something about an uncle."

Uncle Bertram? It was the only relative we had left standing, besides we three siblings. And he wasn't a blood relative, more a close family friend, one whom Mom was terrified of.

I took the phone from Amelia and Flores stepped out of my bedroom to give me some privacy. "Hey, Sparrow. What's up?"

"Hey, Fauna. Is it true Forrest is in town?"

It must be important because he didn't yell at me for using his nickname. "He is, but not for long. Why?"

"Well, Uncle Bertram is in town too, and I thought this sort of coincidence required a family reunion. I'm smoking some ribs on Saturday and would love if y'all could come over."

His hopeful voice almost made me cry. Of all of us, Sparrow was the one who always wanted the Brady Bunch. It was probably why he married the first girl who said yes and started having babies as soon as she would let him. If there was a true father of the year award, Sparrow would earn it.

Too bad I had to crush his dream. "I'm sorry. I don't think now's a good time. Forrest needs to—"

He interrupted me and his stern voice reminded me of Dad's. "Forrest needs to meet his nephews."

He wasn't wrong. Forrest might have made people sick, but he hadn't killed anyone. He could still seek redemption. Those bright, beautiful boys might do him some good. "Okay, I'll convince him to stay a little while longer. He owes me one." Boy, did he owe me one. "Oh, can I bring Amelia and Gina?"

Sparrow scoffed at my request. "Of course, you can. I said it's a family reunion."

My reply caught in my throat as his simple, loving nature cut through all the bullshit we grew up around. "Thanks, Hawke. We'll see you Saturday."

I hung up before I started crying. Pradock was about to come take my picture, a lot. It was bad enough I didn't have any makeup on.

Alone in my bedroom, still a bit shaken from everything that just happened my mind started to spin and even the peace Sparrow's invitation had brought started to shatter.

The last time the whole family was together—minus Dad of course—ended in a huge screaming match between Bertram and Mom. His last words had creeped me out, and I wasn't sorry to see him leave. *I will return when you're ready. Whether your mom likes it or not, you're the one.*

At the time, I'd thought he'd meant those words for Forrest. After all that had happened to me over the last year, I was no longer certain. Had he come back for me? If so, what was I "the one" of exactly?

Chapter Twenty-Nine

Friday after spending a lot of money at Chipped—at cost of course—I was squeezed under a particle board desk resisting the urge to pick off more pieces of the peeling laminate. Amelia threaded a monitor's power cord through the hole in the desk so I could plug it into the surge protector mounted on the wall. We were both anal about cord discipline and refused to leave any of them hanging about willy-nilly.

"Let's fire her up," Amelia said, prompting me to hit the power button on the box as I crawled out from under the desk. She'd mostly forgiven me after I explained what happened. But I wasn't sure it would ever be the same between us.

After running around town to pick up the things we need that I didn't have at Chipped, I'd come back to the shelter to help Amelia install the new donated equipment. Not top of the line, but lightyears beyond what they'd had previously, all six computers were lined up nice and neat in their very own cubicles. The Wi-Fi still needed some upgrades, but at least the wired computers could access the internet reliably. Jacinta said she'd get a list of most frequently used websites, and I'd get them bookmarked for easy access. And Amelia assured us she had an in for some anti-virus software that would update on its own to hopefully keep us from having to come here every week and fix each desktop.

I was kind of enjoying the act of really helping someone. Maybe I'd revamp their menu next.

While Amelia hit next repeatedly to get the software installed, I left to talk to Riko Hernandez. After Heidi healed him and then his sister who wasn't dead at all—another one of Michelle's lies—he'd found a new mission in life. He wanted to heal too. After everything he'd been through, he was ready to move forward and make someone else's life better. We could all learn from Riko.

"Hey, Riko," I said. "The last computer is almost ready, and you'll be able to apply for that housing Gina suggested."

Riko smiled in that full body acceptance he had about himself. "Thanks, Fauna. I already heard back from UHD, and I qualify for government grants to start school as well. I'm going to be a nurse."

I squeezed his shoulder which brought a quiet warmth to my body reflecting his contentment. Maybe someday I'd find some of my own and not have to borrow from others. It really was a good feeling.

But with our family reunion barbecue tomorrow, I doubted I was in for any peace in the near future. Still, it was nice to have family.

Speaking of family, Forrest's laughter came to me from the kitchen, quickly followed by Gina's. Amelia looked up and our eyes met. When hers narrowed, I knew she was thinking the same thing I was: *What is my brother doing flirting with Gina?*

I nodded to let her know I had it handled. Gina might like to save lost puppies, but Forrest was a wolf. I couldn't let him eat her. When I burst into the kitchen like a knight rushing the castle to save the princess, my brother leaned down and kissed someone much shorter than himself. Gina was across the stainless table clasping her hands with a huge smile on her face. If I didn't know where we were, I'd think she was watching the ending of a sweet romance. We do let her pick our girl night movies sometimes, and I'd seen that expression more than once.

Yet, if my brother wasn't kissing Gina, who was he ...? A sidestep showed me the truth. It was the healer.

Shock vibrated in my voice. "Heidi?"

She blinked and pulled back from Forrest, though he still pressed her body against his. "Hey, Fauna." She sounded weak but happy.

I got close enough that the waves of love from Heidi warmed my muscles. She still loved him. How could she forgive him for what he made her do? Maybe it wasn't my place to question her. But I couldn't help myself. "Do we need to talk?"

Gina interrupted, "Oh stop it, Fauna. Can't you see they're in love. I mean, you have to *feel* it. I do, and I'm not an empath."

Wow, even Gina was mad at me. Everything was going great. "Actually, I can feel it from Heidi, but ..."

Forrest sighed like he was some sort of martyr dealing with a doubting follower again. "This is between me and Heidi. She's the only one who has to believe me."

Heidi pushed Forrest back slightly so she could face me straight on. Her grayish skin showed she was still healing people at the hospital. It was a much slower process now, especially since she refused to let me help. "Forrest definitely fucked up, but he didn't kill anyone, and trust me when I say you can draw out someone's energy until there is none left." The shadow that crossed her face, as well as the heartburn that bubbled up my throat, confessed her personal experience with that.

As he turned to face me, Forrest moved his arm up around Heidi's shoulders and kept her close. "I didn't know when Heidi recharged like that, that the victims wouldn't recover on their own like she did. That's why I only chose healthy people. I thought they'd get better, just slowly, while Heidi was free to keep healing, which she loves more than anything."

"Almost anything." Heidi leaned her head against his shoulder and Forrest kissed the top of it. "We're heading up to Dallas once I've finished with these patients. I'm not leaving anyone behind."

Amelia popped through the door, her anxiety made my head crawl. She really couldn't resist her protective nature. When she spotted Forrest and Heidi in each other's arms, my scalp calmed, and Amelia moved to Gina's side of the table with her eyebrow raised. Gina nodded with a huge smile on her face. That girl really did love love.

I tried to ignore the fact that I stood alone. "How are you going to get in to see those patients? No one is going to believe the truth, even Tucker isn't sure what's happening, he just trusts the results."

"Oh, that was all Forrest's genius plan." Heidi's pride barely made a dent in my instant suspicion.

My arms crossed simultaneously with Amelia's. At least, we were still in sync with some things. "Did he now? And what was his genius plan?"

Forrest puffed out his chest. "You can scoff all you want, but I'm good with the plans."

"I'm well aware. Never a doubt. I'm just waiting for the twist and who gets to be the victim this time."

Heidi pushed off from Forrest as he and I prepared to go at it. "That's enough, you two. Forrest suggested that the entire illness was psychosomatic which is why it wasn't contagious and they couldn't find a disease vector in anyone's blood."

"Huh," was the best reply I could come up with.

Amelia begrudgingly admitted. "Okay, that was pretty ingenious."

Forrest bowed his head in fake humility. "So Dr. Wickman called the Dallas hospital and told them the same thing and that each had come down with it after one of our rallies, which is true. So Heidi can see them one at a time until she convinces them there's nothing wrong."

Heidi continued, "With the evidence of the recovery of the patients here in Houston, Dallas has agreed to let us try."

For some reason, the thought of them leaving before I really got to work through my feelings over what happened between Forrest and I made me sad. I wanted a tidy ending. I supposed wants are just that and never tidy.

"Are you coming back?" I asked, trying not to sound too vulnerable.

Nevertheless, Gina sensed the impending family discussion. "Amelia, how are those computers coming along? Are you ready for that list of frequently used sites?"

Amelia hesitated for only a moment before heading toward the door. "And Jacinta said we should probably put up a porn blocker."

Gina nodded as she disappeared behind Amelia into the cafeteria. "Oh for sure. You never know what these volunteers will get up to." She winked at me as the door closed behind her.

Heidi moved forward and grasped both of my hands. "It's been a pleasure getting to know you, Fauna. When Forrest and I decide on our permanent mission, we'll be back to Houston to tell you first."

I flinched for a moment as some of my energy wanted to instinctively refill her drained "soul" as she called it. I still hadn't given it a name. I wasn't sure I believed in a soul. "I look forward to that day."

She smiled back at Forrest as she left for the cafeteria. I heard some chants of "Healer" as some of the people recognized her.

I gestured toward the door. "You should probably go after her before she's mobbed."

"She can handle herself." He held out his arms to me. "And I want a hug."

Why did I want to cry right now? A little over a week ago, the last thing I'd wanted to see was my older brother and now I was sad about him leaving. How did he do this to me? I gave in and he folded me in his arms. Though it was still weird to not feel his emotions, it was somehow comforting to smell his unique odor and feel the strong, yet gentle squeeze of his arms and to feel loved in a way I had to trust instead of verify.

"Hey, Fauna?" The hesitation in his voice hinted at another confession.

I pulled back to look at his face. "Yes?"

"Sparrow told me Uncle Bertram is staying in town for a while. Something about work responsibilities, though I have no idea what he does for a living."

"That's what I heard too. You're going to the barbecue tomorrow, right?"

"Heidi and I will make an appearance." Forrest rubbed my arms. "But in case we can't talk freely, I want you to be careful around him. Mom was terrified of Bertram, and she could never quite tell me why. But I've always suspected he had something to do with Dad's death."

"What?" I didn't know where to start.

Tucker pushed through the kitchen door. "Hey, beautiful," he said with his easy charm and his happiness at seeing me tickled my fingers and toes. "Gina said you were in here. Are you ready for lunch?"

"We'll talk about it later." Forrest kissed me on the forehead and walked out the door.

Easily brushing aside Forrest's warning, I focused on Tucker. "Never been more ready." I ran my fingertips up his arm. "Wanna eat at your place?"

His cheeks flushed as my nipples tingled with the reaction I successfully elicited. "I'll never say no to 'lunch at my place.'" He gave me a passionate kiss that made every inch of my skin tingle. I moaned in protest when he pulled away. "But you owe me an explanation. I'm not buying the psychosomatic bullshit even though I sold it pretty heavily to my colleagues. Whatever it was that I experienced wasn't caused by my brain."

There was always one more shoe. "I will tell you everything, but first lunch."

He didn't argue anymore as we slipped out the back entrance hand in hand.

A FREE STORY FROM KELLY LYNN COLBY'S BRAIN

Join Kelly's newsletter and keep up with all of her adventurers. She can't wait to take you along for the ride. With a new YA fantasy in progress, an alternative history in the research phase, book three in her paranormal series in the writing stage, and always a new short story or two waiting to jump out at her unsuspecting brain, there's always something exciting going on.

Acknowledgments

First, I have to thank my accountability group. Without you, I might never have finished this manuscript. Jessica Raney, JoAnna Jordan, and Ann Rose are stellar writers in their own right and I'm honored to be among their company.

Stefanie Saw yet again created an incredible cover as the first thing readers see before they dive into Fauna's drama. I'm so grateful I discovered her website six years ago. Talent like hers is hard to find.

S.G. George is the best copy editor anyone could ask for. She even recognized a bad writing habit of mine which will help me write stronger prose in the future.

My family is the most supportive group of people. My husband has full force jumped into this writing/publishing world and always encourages me to do that next thing. My kids have helped us pack up books, run booths, and house sat while we worked conventions out of town. My moms, Pam and Vicky, brag about what we do and support us like super fans. I couldn't do any of this without them.

Lastly, I want to thank the writing communities at Superstars Writing Seminar and Dragon Con. Because of all of you, I have this incredible career where I get to make stuff up and other people like to read about it. It's insane and I love it.

Kelly Lynn Colby owns one hat, but wears many. She's a writer of epic fantasy (The Recharging) and paranormal thrillers (Emergence), a freelance editor, a publisher, and a podcaster. As the Editorial Director and Publisher at Cursed Dragon Ship Publishing, Kelly is privileged to work with a plethora of speculative fiction writers. She decided everyone else should get to know them as well, so she started "20 Questions with your Favorite Author" every Tuesday. By adding "Writing Wrongs" on Monday nights—a D&D adventure where all the players are writers—she's now fully committed to this podcast hat. When she's not hogging the mic, Kelly writes and edits and answers an inordinate number of emails at her cluttered desk, coffee shops, and parks, mostly in Houston, Texas. You can follow her adventures on her blog at kellylynncolby.com.

facebook.com/kcolbywrites
twitter.com/kcolbywrites
instagram.com/kcolbywrites

Also by Kelly Lynn Colby

Missed Book One? Check out *The Collector* and see how Fauna's journey began.

A curse can be a gift until it makes you the target of a sadistic killer.

Also by Kelly Lynn Colby

When magic is rediscovered in a land devoid of it, the royal twins must compete to earn the right to be called True Heir, a title that means more than either imagined.

CPSIA information can be obtained
at www.ICGtesting.com
Printed in the USA
BVHW051237041122
651158BV00004B/891